# EMBRACE THE FLAME

## A RAVEN CRAWFORD SIBLING STORY

J. C. McKenzie

**"Do I even want to know what's going on?"**
A familiar voice broke through the sounds of nature.

Juni whipped around in time to watch Bane step from his portal of horrors. Rourke and Lincoln moved to block her with their bodies.

Bane's arrival had not surprised them. They always had her back.

Bane gave Lincoln a scathing look—up and down, before turning away dismissively. Annoyance pinged along their bond.

His reaction to Rourke was much more interesting, and confusing. She received a spattering of emotions—surprise, anger, and hurt.

Hurt?

Before she could probe the bond for more information, he clamped down on his feelings and all she got was ice.

Fine then.

"A fae, a reg, and a shifter were alone in the forest." Bane peered around Rourke's hulking body to pin her with his dark gaze. "There's a joke in there somewhere."

He was the joke, but she didn't have a human mouth to snap back at him. Instead, she sent irritation through their bond, but it hit the emotional blockade he'd built.

Bane smirked and turned to Lincoln. "I guess the punchline must be you."

# BOOKS BY J. C. MCKENZIE

## *The Lark Morgan Series (forthcoming)*

Death Maker

Death Raiser

Death Taker

Death Stealer

## *Isle and Eyrie Series*

Cormorant Run

Heir of the Eyrie

## *House of Moon and Stars*

The Night House

House of Chaos

## *Crawford Investigations*

Conspiracy of Ravens

Nevermore

Queen of Corvids

The Call of Corvids

From the Shadows

Into the Fire

Dark Legacy

Embrace the Flame

### The Carus Series

Shift Happens

Beast Coast

Carpe Demon

Shift Work

Beast of All

### Obsidian Flame

Dangerous Dreams

Dangerous Liaisons

Dangerous Decisions

### That Old Black Magic

The Good Griffin

### Standalones

Immortal Throne (with Harper A. Brooks)

Call of the Deep (The Shucker's Booktique)

Stormbound (Be My Love)

## PRAISE FOR J. C. MCKENZIE'S BOOKS

*Conspiracy of Ravens*
"Raven is my kind of people. Half hot-mess, half bad-ass, all awesome... the story had plenty of humor, action and mystery rolled up in a nice paced story."
~ Urban Fantasy Investigations

*Nevermore*
"The dramas, dangers, intrigue, and tension of *Nevermore* will have you glued to the pages, and when it is finished, Ms. McKenzie will have left you satisfied yet wanting more."
~ Fresh Fiction

*Queen of Corvids*
"It has all the classic comedy, angst, and drama that I have come to expect from J.C. McKenzie, and then it piles on mystery and more interesting characters."
~ Lady with a Quill

*The Call of Corvids*
"This is a fascinating read that brings together a world that has been marred with fae wars"
~ Fresh Fiction

This is a work of fiction. Names, characters, places, and incidents are either the product of the author's imagination or are used fictitiously, and any resemblance to actual persons living or dead, business establishments, events, or locales, is entirely coincidental.

**Embrace the Flame**

Contact Information: jcmckenzie@jcmckenzie.ca

Cover Art: Eerilyfair Design

Publishing History:

First JCM Publications Edition, 2022

Rituals & Runes Boxset, 2022

ISBN: 978-1-990143-19-9 (print)

ISBN: 978-1-990143-20-5 (ebook)

*To my talented cover artist, Anna L. Spies,*

*Thank you for all the gorgeous covers*

"When does a joke become a dad joke?"
(Dramatic pause)
"When it's full groan."

— JUNI'S DAD

# CHAPTER 1

"Why do girls walk in 3s, 5s and 7s?"
(Dramatic pause)
"Because they *can't even.*"

— JUNI'S DAD

Juni Crawford stared at the plaque mounted on the log cabin wall and contemplated stabbing her host in the neck. And not for the first time. Her thoughts had a recurring violent nature, all centred on her "host."

Bane, the Lord of War, sat across from her on a cushy sofa. He wore jeans, combat boots and a long-sleeved Henley. Despite the fairly normal clothes, the sheer ferocity of his presence gave him away as a feared dark fae lord. He wasn't fooling anyone with the mortal clothing, so he must wear it because he actually liked it.

Nothing about Bane made sense.

Despite the summer month, the air outside was cool. A roaring fire bathing them in heat and its fiery glow. Her fox shifting senses took in every minute detail of the cabin while her mind reeled from events of the other night. She'd bound herself to this jerk to unlock her light fae powers and rescue Lincoln, her friend. Her more-than-a-friend.

Totally worth it, but now she had to deal with the consequences.

Currently, said consequence narrowed his eyes at her. "You can't kill me."

"I'll find a way." She folded her arms.

He'd mentioned her inability to hurt him more than once, almost as if he could read her mind, or had legitimate concerns about her potentially losing it.

She shuddered.

The idea of Bane in her head made her stomach twist into a knot.

So far, the big bad dark fae lord hadn't done anything aside from feed her tacos and take her to this creepy cabin.

She'd almost forgive him for all this crap for the tacos alone.

Almost.

They were that good.

She glanced at the plaque again. Its sprawling

script mocking her as it read, "Life is better at the cabin."

She sank back in her seat, her mind drifting to her family. She'd give anything to be at home right now listening to one of Dad's god-awful jokes. Her fingers itched to press the enchanted stone on her choker to call her family here. One touch, one thought, and her family could form a portal to pop into this cabin and take her away.

Or die trying.

What if calling her family was exactly what Bane wanted? He never did things the straight-forward way. He made plans in an intricate, overlapping web, hiding more devious goals behind fairly inane actions. What else could explain what he'd done? He'd agreed to unlock her light fae divinity in exchange for her becoming his *caomhnóir*. Pronounced something like "keev-noy-r," the fae bond made her his guardian for life. No one who knew Juni would peg her for good guardian material. Taking orders wasn't exactly something she excelled in.

But Bane didn't bond Juni for Juni. He did it so her life would become inextricably bound to his. And now, because of the bond, Juni's sister, the Queen of Corvids, couldn't kill Bane without also killing Juni.

She'd really messed up.

It didn't help that Bane had taken to calling her his insurance policy.

"I can tell you're still debating how to kill me. You

keep stroking that magical pouch that holds your weapons," Bane said. "It seems you have a lot to learn about being a guardian."

"Not my fault you opted for the latest Crawford Model," she said. "Put in a complaint. We're still working out the bugs."

Bane smirked and leaned back to close his eyes. "Have you tried playing with your power yet?"

She scowled at him, even though he wouldn't see it.

The man was a walking innuendo. If she were the type of woman attracted to a death trap, which she wasn't, these one-liners of Bane's might actually work on her, especially paired with his dark fae good looks.

Many would consider Bane attractive.

Not Juni.

She had another man on her mind. A reg. A human male without any supernatural abilities who'd sacrificed his life to save her.

In return, she'd sacrificed her freedom to save him and ended up bonded to Bane and hanging out in his cabin. That wasn't all she'd given up. Her fingers itched to open her magical pouch and confirm the wish-granting orb was truly gone. She'd used it to have Inari, a light fae god and her great-grandmother, heal Lincoln.

What was he doing right now?

Her stomach sunk. Odin's shriveled nuggets. He

probably faced the firing squad that made up her family.

They'd be terrible.

Nothing existed in the Mortal Realm more terrifying than her parents' disappointment or Raven's wrath.

Another thought struck her, and dread shimmied down her spine. They better not hurt Lincoln. Especially after she went to all that trouble to keep him alive.

Juni tightened her grip on her dagger.

At least she got to say goodbye before Bane hauled her off to the Underworld. Her lips still tingled from Lincoln's kiss, and her skin warmed with the thought of him holding her.

"Please stop thinking about that reg." Bane shifted in his seat and popped open his eyes.

"Uncomfortable?" Though Bane couldn't read her mind, at least not that she knew of, he could sense her feelings and emotions through their bond.

"Very."

"Sorry, not sorry." She sat back. "Deal with it."

To add salt to the wound, she let her mind drift to thoughts of Lincoln. When they were teenagers, he'd betrayed her and broke her heart. That should've been the end of their story, but he'd spent six years atoning for his mistake. She'd taken longer than she cared to admit to realize the truth of her feelings for the mortal human. She didn't just tolerate him. She loved him.

Instead of thinking about the direness of her circumstances, she thought of Lincoln's mouth on hers, his hands exploring her body.

Bane growled and leaned forward. "I know you're attempting to annoy me, but that's not the effect you're having. All I sense from the bond is how horny you are."

Oh no.

"How ready." His dark gaze bled out, so his eyes appeared entirely black.

Eyes of the underworld, like those of her two oldest siblings. The black from Bane's irises bled into the whites—a sure sign of a dark fae. Bane and his lot got their name because they originated from the Underworld prior to the barrier collapse between realms. Though they had vastly different physical appearances, they were all devastating to look at and manipulated potent magic. The easiest way to identify dark fae aristocracy was by looking at their eyes. They "bled out" to turn completely black when a dark fae experienced intense emotion or wielded a lot of power.

"So now," Bane continued. "I'm alone, in a cabin, with an attractive, horny woman who's sending all sorts of naughty feelings. I feel what you feel." He paused. "Do you understand?"

"I'm horny so now you're horny?"

"Exactly."

Argh. Definitely not the effect she wanted.

"So unless you want me to act on those feelings

and relieve some of the tension, I suggest you cut it out."

"You wouldn't."

Something flashed in his gaze. "I will never force you to do anything you don't want to do."

Somehow, he didn't make that sound reassuring.

Lincoln had once said Bane was only known for two things—fighting and fucking.

Juni clamped her mouth shut, folded her arms over her chest and looked away.

Bane chuckled.

He'd won this round, but Juni planned to play the long game. If she excelled at anything, it was annoying her family. Now, she had the opportunity to flex her skills on an unwilling participant. Juni would get out of this bond somehow, and then she'd relish bringing down the Lord of War.

# CHAPTER 2

"Why couldn't the bicycle stand up by itself?"
(Dramatic pause)
"It was two-tired."

— JUNI'S DAD

A familiar energy vibrated the air and made the hairs on the back of her neck stand up. Portal magic. Someone was forming a portal into Bane's personal cabin, and only a few people had the magical means to accomplish the task.

No!

They couldn't come here. She sat up and wildly searched the room. Bane didn't have a legion of warriors hiding out in the closet, nor had she detected any traps, but that didn't mean Bane hadn't planned something.

He was sneaky like that.

Four people materialized in the small living room. Her sister Raven, the Queen of Corvids; Cole Camhanaich, her brother-in-law and lord of shadows; Rourke, her sister's guardian.

And Lincoln.

The sight of him, alive and healthy stole her breath away.

When they were teenagers, the softness of youth had rounded Lincoln's cheeks. He'd had an easy smile, and a twinkle of mischief in his gaze. Then he'd betrayed her and spent time in her sister's dungeon. Those years and Rourke's training had hardened him in the most delicious way. Gaze fierce, expression stern, the softness gone.

If she didn't know better, she'd mistake him for one of the many deadly fae warriors in her sister's court. He wore a fitted, black leather vest with studded plates, leather vambraces to protect his forearms and dark pants tucked into armoured boots that reached his knees. Every inch of him looked dark fae.

But Lincoln wasn't fae.

He was all human.

And all hers.

"Ah, just like old times," Bane crooned from where he lay sprawled on the couch by the fire.

Juni folded her arms over her chest and waited for

the theatrics to start.

But oddly, they didn't.

Raven turned her attention from Bane and focused on Juni. Her older sister opted for the leather armour favoured by fae for stealth and increased mobility instead of the battle bra she normally wore. Maybe she'd finally grown tired of her family making fun of her attire, even if it made sense why she should wear it.

Raven's familiar scent wound around her. The playful mischief smell comforting, familiar, but also different.

Juni sat up in her seat and drew in more of the scent. Warmth spread through her body. There was only one thing that could change her sister's scent like this, but now was not the time to ask her about it.

Raven had always been striking. Tall and fit with curves, flawless skin and pouty lips, Juni couldn't remember a time when she didn't envy her older sister. Raven had grown into a fierce, independent woman, and she'd found Cole. That man lived for her sister and the two of them gave off serious couple goals.

Raven's dark gaze scanned Juni's unruly mane, no doubt taking in what an absurd clusterfuck it was and grimaced. "Are you okay?"

"I'm the farthest thing from okay," Juni said. Like, honestly? What was okay about this situation? Her sister shouldn't be here. Juni got herself in this mess, and she could dig her own way out.

Raven went back and forth from studying Juni to

scrutinizing Bane, her frown deepening with each movement. Finally, she pulled herself more upright and tightened her grip on the scythe, turning her knuckles white. "Tell me what you want and release my sister."

Juni would know that stubborn look anywhere. Probably not the time to point out how Raven's frowning would cause wrinkles or that she should go home and rest.

"I already told you what I want." Bane remained relaxed and calm in the chair.

"If I drop the barrier, you'll release Juni?" Raven narrowed her eyes at the Lord of War.

No. No way. Raven couldn't possibly consider giving into this lunatic's demands. Juni wasn't worth it. Nobody was. He'd never stop.

"Why would I do that?" Bane asked. "She's my insurance policy, my only guarantee you'll do as I ask and not kill me at the first possibility."

"I'll swear a fae oath," Raven offered without hesitation.

A fae oath bound the participants with their lives. It was irrevocable and concrete. Swearing a fae oath to refrain from harming Bane without adding any stipulations or perimeters would leave Raven incredibly vulnerable. No fae would swear such an oath unless the situation was dire.

Juni and Raven might have their sisterly spats, but Juni never doubted her older half-sibling's love for her.

Raven's lack of hesitation to once again place herself in harm's way to protect Juni validated everything she felt for her sister. But Raven shouldn't have to do this. She never should've had to do any of it.

Juni shook her head. Raven couldn't make this sacrifice. Juni wouldn't allow it.

Neither would Cole. Her brother-in-law growled, obviously not liking the idea of Raven swearing an oath any more than Juni did. Cole would wrap Raven in bubble wrap if her sister allowed it, and Raven most definitely wouldn't allow it.

As the daddy of assassin's guild, Cole Camhanaich radiated danger and death. When she'd first met him, she didn't know whether she should swoon in his arms or tuck tail and run. She'd been a very angsty, easily impressionable teenager, but that didn't mean Cole was any less impressive now than the day she first met him.

His dark hair contrasted sharply with his smooth pale skin, and his eyes always flashed when he looked at Raven. Cole loved her sister on a level Juni only hoped to obtain.

Watching Cole cringe and tense every time Raven asserted her independence while doing something stupid had become a favourite Crawford family event.

Juni opened her mouth to protest Raven's offer at the same time Cole stepped forward, looking intent on physically removing Raven from the situation.

Raven waved them off.

"Not good enough," Bane said. "You've proven quite adept at working around the restrictions of an oath already."

He had a point.

Raven had made Bane a promise in the past to construct a barrier. Because of a loophole in the wording, though, Raven met her end of the bargain in a way that prevented Bane from using the barrier to his advantage as intended. And his master plans for world domination crumbled down around him.

"I don't understand." Raven frowned harder.

That made two of them. If Bane didn't want a fae oath, what the heck did he want?

"Probably not the first time that's happened," Bane quipped, looking smug enough to throat punch.

"Why would Raven grant your wish if you're not willing to release Juni?" Cole asked. The man could only control his protective nature so much when Raven's safety was in question.

Cole, Raven, and Bane started arguing back and forth while Rourke remained silent and watchful.

Juni snuck another glance at Lincoln while the grown-ups bickered. Yeah, sure. She was an adult, too. But these were adulting adults.

Her heart ached. She wanted to get up from this spot and launch herself at Lincoln. Her sister and brother-in-law would never let her live it down, but she didn't care. Lincoln watched her, his expression unreadable, his gaze unwavering. He'd had years of perfecting his stone statue impersonation. He wore that mask every time he wanted to hide his feelings.

He hadn't taken his gaze off her since they arrived. The voices of the others washed over her as she maintained the eye contact. Somehow, the connection with Lincoln relaxed her, centering her in her position.

"So I don't make the queen's little sister's life miserable," Bane said, answering something Cole had asked.

Wait. That was her. She really should pay attention.

As difficult as she found it, with a herculean effort, she tore her gaze away from Lincoln once again. Maybe Bane would permit visitors. Conjugal visits. That sort of thing.

"You're making all our lives miserable," Raven pointed out. "You didn't need my sister as your caomh-nóir to accomplish that. Cut the crap. You won't harm her, and we won't kill you, so we're at a stalemate as far as threats of torture, maiming and murder go."

"Could've just said bodily harm." Rourke finally broke his silence. And, of course, he'd done so to poke fun at her sister.

Wearing full fae armour with black matte metal and a cape draped around him like shadows, Rourke looked every inch the dangerous assassin. A weapon-warping dark fae, Rourke had been Juni's saviour and mentor for years. She'd had a raging crush on him when she was younger, but her feelings had evolved into a friendship and deep respect.

"What are you offering?" Bane straightened in his seat, gaze calculating. He was up to something. Juni was only a means to an end, she understood that, but how did he plan to use her? Nobody, including her, believed for one second he needed Juni as a caomhnóir.

"I'll give you what you want," Raven said. "But the price is releasing Juni."

"No deal," Bane said.

"Then ask for something else, but just know I won't trade for anything less."

Juni froze, her emotions waffling between warm, fuzzy love and bone-chilling fear. Bane could ask for anything, and her sister would agree.

Her spine stiffened.

Juni couldn't let that happen. She wouldn't let her sister make any more sacrifices, especially not for her.

Bane grinned and didn't even bother trying to hide it. That never boded well. "I'm sure I'll think of something."

Rat bastard. Guaranteed he knew precisely what he wanted. He had to continue moving the chess pieces around the board first, though. He must be waiting for something else to fall in place.

"You know how to reach me," Raven said. "In the meantime, Juni's coming with us."

Juni held her breath. Would he let her go? Her heart threatened to burst from her chest.

Bane laughed, that nauseating bellow that told anyone listening he found the current situation highly amusing. It just made her want to stab him. Her fingers itched to grab the hilt of her dagger.

Bane reached into his pocket and pulled out a small gray lodestone, the one she used to get here, and tossed it at her. She caught it easily, the stone now a familiar cold surface. When had he recharged it? He said it was single use, and she'd already used it. Or had he misled her somehow? Or did he just have a basket of these in some storage closet?

Juni gave up trying to figure him out. Keeping her eyes on the Lord of War, she got to her feet and walked across the room to stand by her sister. Thankfully, her legs didn't buckle.

Lincoln held his hand out and without hesitation, she slipped her hand into his. She leaned into him, enjoying his strength and familiar scent.

"You may have your sister," Bane said as he stood. "Juni could use some training in fae magic and manners while you're at it."

Juni turned and flipped up her middle finger to wave goodbye and wasn't surprised to find her sister had done the exact same thing.

Great minds think alike, after all.

Cole wrapped his shadows around the group and carried them away, but not before Bane's gaze locked on hers. They bled out to full fae black, a silent promise sparking in his gaze.

He might've let her go for now, but he'd be back.

# CHAPTER 3

"Your Mom told me to do lunges to stay in shape."
(Dramatic pause)
"That would be a big step forward."

— JUNI'S DAD

Juni stepped from the portal made from her brother-in-law's swirling shadows and let the summer's warm night air flow over her. She stood in the back alley behind her childhood home. Everyone else had moved away except Lincoln. He remained by her side, still holding her hand.

"Go inside," Raven commanded.

Normally, Juni would put up a fight on principle. Just because Raven was over a decade older than her didn't mean she could boss Juni around.

Juni was a fierce, independent woman.

And she was so, so tired.

No amount of delay would prevent the lecture from Mom and Dad that waited inside, either. If she ripped off the bandage maybe she'd finally get to relax for the first time in days.

Lincoln squeezed her hand.

With a nod, she walked away from her sister and headed toward the house.

"I'll go with them," Cole said somewhere behind her.

She sighed in relief. She hadn't had the opportunity to find out what happened while she was gone, so she didn't know if her parents' feelings about Lincoln had changed from mild distrust to outright hate, but they probably still harboured resentment toward him for the role he played in her abduction six years ago.

But they loved Cole.

Adored him.

He might be the patron fae of assassins and dangerous as fuck, but he might as well be a unicorn plush toy or a beloved golden retriever as far as they were concerned. In Mom and Dad's eyes, Cole could do no wrong. His presence would soften the impending lecture.

"You ready?" Lincoln looked down at her, the moonlight glinting off his dark gaze.

"About as ready as I'll ever be," she replied.

He opened the backdoor and stood to the side so she could enter first.

As expected, Mom and Dad sat at the dining table, hands clasped in front of them. They would've seen her walking up from the fence gate leading from the alley. Dad didn't spout off one of his dad jokes at first sight, so something was definitely wrong.

Instead of launching into a tirade about her life choices, Mom choked back a sob, leapt from her seat and enveloped Juni in a giant hug.

A grunt and a few footsteps later, Dad's arms circled them both.

"You said you wouldn't make a scene," Dad mumbled into her hair at Mom.

"Shut up, Terry." Mom sniffed.

Juni let go of Lincoln's hand to hug them back.

"We were so worried," Mom said.

"We love you so much, Junebug," Dad said.

Not quite the welcome she'd expected. Her chest grew warm. Her lungs constricted. She squeezed her parents. Not too long ago, she'd wondered when, if ever, she'd see them again. Her eyes stung, and she desperately blinked back tears.

Over Mom's shoulder, she caught Cole's gaze. He stood stoically by the exit monitoring the situation inside, but he also kept glancing outside. Something must be going on in the alley. Enough to make him tense and rest his hand on his sword hilt, but not enough for him to charge out there or sift through the shadows to help Raven.

Cole had come a long way over the years in trusting Raven to take care of her own business, but, obviously, that didn't stop him from worrying.

Obsessive and possessive, she didn't envy anyone who tried to get in the way of Cole's relationship with Raven. He manipulated shadows. They acted as his blades, fists, ears, and shields. Right now, Juni wished he would somehow use his special powers to help her avoid the uncomfortable conversation that would undoubtedly unfold.

"How could you make such a monumentally stupid decision?" Mom asked while trying to smooth down Juni's wild mane. To anyone from the outside looking in, they'd assume Mom referred to her hair, now more of a bird's nest than anything remotely fashionable.

Juni sighed. She couldn't delay the inevitable any longer. They'd returned to the regularly scheduled program.

Mom and Dad released her, and she stepped back. "I determined the price worth it. I regret nothing."

Lincoln shifted his weight from foot to foot where he stood beside her. His cheeks gained a pinkish tinge, and he pulled at the collar of his shirt when he cleared his throat. "Now's probably a good time to mention that your entire family knows we kissed."

"Why on Earth would you tell them that?" she asked.

Oh. My. God.

They'd tease her relentlessly and mercilessly now.

Was Mike sitting upstairs in his room right now, cackling gleefully while he compiled a list of insults?

Wait a minute.

"Where is Mike?" she asked.

"Working on a case," Dad answered. "He'll be upset that he missed this."

Probably for the best her brother wasn't in attendance. Her family knew she'd made out with Lincoln, and, for some reason, he thought now was a good time to bring it all up.

Her cheeks grew warm, probably matching Lincoln's blush. "Exactly how did you slip our kiss into a conversation?"

"Well, from the sound of it, you're the one who did the slipping," Dad grumbled.

What? "What?"

Dad waved his hand in the air. "You know..." He leaned in. "Slipping the tongue? Don't you kids still say that?"

Dead. She was officially dead. And mortification would be listed as the cause of death.

"They couldn't figure out how I got trapped in a spell when it was set for you." Lincoln's face had gone from pink to a deep red. "They figured it out."

Her tongue in Lincoln's mouth had been enough to trigger Hikaru's spell. Instead of just Juni, they both ended up transported to a remote location for the kitsune to exact his revenge.

"Honestly, dear. You should keep your tongue to yourself," Mom said. "In your own mouth."

Juni groaned and ran her hand down her face. "Of all people to lecture me on body parts, Mom, I don't think you're qualified." They all knew Mom had a wild past.

Mom rocked back on her heels, her head jerking back as if Juni had slapped her.

"We've all heard your stories about your single days," Juni added quickly before her own mother was listed as her COD instead of mortification.

"Which is exactly why I'm perfectly equipped to provide this little chat." Mom lifted her chin.

Oh dear, no. Mom better not launch into a lecture and the birds and the bees. She'd barely survived the last one.

Juni flung her hands in the air. "I'm twenty-one years old. I'm allowed to kiss the boy I like, and I'm allowed to use my tongue."

The room instantly went quiet.

Lincoln's blush had disappeared. He watched her intently, his gaze flashing with a promise.

Oh my.

"I'll be right back," Cole said.

"Traitor." Juni ripped her gaze away from Lincoln in time to watch Cole disappear in a swirl of shadow.

Cole couldn't have wanted to miss out on this conversation. Raven must've concluded her business outside. Knowing Cole, he couldn't resist checking in with her. That meant they had a few minutes before he returned.

"Anyway." She turned to her parents. "Are we going to talk about the change in Raven's scent?"

Mom's face broke into a wide grin that threatened to split her face in two.

"We're going to pretend we don't know," Dad said, glancing outside.

"What?" Juni straightened. "Why?"

"Because she hasn't said anything, dear." Mom grew serious. "Just because we can detect private matters doesn't mean they're any less private."

Right. Mom had given her that lecture more than a few times growing up. As a fox shifter, her sense of smell picked up all sorts of details—what someone last ate, what soap they used, who they slept with...all sorts of details. Normally, she catalogued the information and moved on.

But this...

This was Raven.

Her tormentor and saviour. Her role model. Her queen.

Though Raven hadn't teased Juni as mercilessly as

Mike, she'd definitely contributed. And now it was payback time.

Except Mom was saying it wasn't payback time.

Was she too old to pout?

"Not fair," she said.

Mom raised an eyebrow. "Exactly how old are you again?"

Juni clamped her mouth shut and ignored Lincoln's questioning gaze. As a reg, without any heightened senses, he had no idea what they discussed, but he didn't have a chance to ask.

Mom and Dad exchanged a look and spent the next half an hour or so grilling her about everything that had happened in the last seventy-two hours.

"It was still monumentally stupid," Mom muttered after Juni explained the sacrifices she made to save Lincoln's life. In front of Lincoln.

Because that wasn't awkward.

Raven chose that precise moment to walk into the house, Rourke and Cole close behind her. She narrowed her dark fae gaze at Juni and raised her hand, waving her pointer finger at Juni, then Lincoln, then back at her again.

"You two," Raven said. "Basement. Now."

"We weren't done," Mom said.

Raven looked at Mom and stilled. "I need information to protect the family and the Corvid Court."

"Fine." Mom blew a strand of hair from her face.

Juni didn't wait for Mom to reconsider. She

instantly turned to the stairs that led to her basement bedroom.

Without saying a word, Lincoln walked with her.

They were both too tired to put up a fight and given her sister, the Queen of Corvids, breathed down their necks as they descended into the dark basement, maybe they should have.

# CHAPTER 4

"Why do three and five make such a great team?"
(Dramatic pause)
"Because they always ate together."

— JUNI'S DAD

J uni sat on the edge of the bed beside Lincoln, their thighs pressed together, and their hands clasped.

She would've preferred to stare into Lincoln's beautiful eyes but instead, she kept her focus on her sister who currently wore a path in the carpet with her pacing. What was Raven's problem?

Besides the whole bonding to her mortal enemy and creating an extra layer of complexity to her reign that she didn't need...

Hmm...

Juni swallowed, and Raven stopped to point at them again. "When did this happen?"

Juni squeezed Lincoln's hand and lifted her chin. Her relationship with Lincoln had barely started before Bane whisked her off to that cabin.

"It's new," Juni answered. "Don't ruin it."

Raven scowled, her striking features twisting. "Why would I do that?"

"Well, I don't know," Juni said. "But you've been pacing in front of us for the last ten minutes, and you're starting to freak me out. Now you're facing off with us like you're about to scold us for being naughty children. I already have parents, thank you very much."

Though Juni had gotten off lightly from the parental lecture thanks to Raven, she'd never admit it.

"I'm not going to scold you," Raven said. "I want to know what the fuck is going on."

Lincoln squeezed Juni's hand to reassure her. Or maybe it was a warning.

"I know Inari is our great-grandmother," Raven continued. "You left that part out about your trip to the Realm of Light, by the way."

On one of Juni's last cases, she'd discovered Inari, the kami of grains, harvest, and agriculture was their maternal great-grandmother. That had been a lovely surprise with ramifications she hadn't had a chance to process yet. Inari had also gifted Juni with the wish-granting hōju she'd ultimately used to save Lincoln's life.

"I didn't have the opportunity to speak with you privately. I figured I had time to tell you later," Juni explained. Of course, things hadn't worked out that way.

"Like a text message wouldn't work?" Raven's sarcasm practically dripped from her naturally pouty lips.

Growing up, Juni idolized Raven. She'd wanted her sister's dark, sultry looks instead of the gingersnap ones she got. Accepting her own rat's nest hair and pasty complexion hadn't been easy as a teenager. Now she loved their differences and had grown to appreciate her own unique beauty.

As Dad said, so often when they were growing up, "You can't have the night without the sun, and the sun isn't nearly as impressive unless it follows the darkness."

He might've been referring to something else, but whatever. Juni took it to mean Mike and her embodied sunlight while Raven and Bear, the dark fae twins, represented the night.

In retrospect, the idea was a little too on the nose with their light fae heritage.

"Mike's not the only one who can hack into messages," Juni explained, focusing back on the conversation with her sister. "I try to avoid sending life-altering information in text as much as possible. I wanted to keep the information about the hōju private. Not from the family, but everyone else. I'd just had someone try to kill me for it and didn't know what other people would do if they found out I possessed a hōju or discovered Inari was our great-grandmother."

Her words made Raven pause, which helped Juni to control the sinking sensation in her stomach.

Juni had liked Hikaru, she'd kissed him, and he'd turned around and betrayed her the first chance he got. He'd tried to steal the magical gift, and he nearly killed Lincoln in the process.

And now, Lincoln sat perfectly healthy beside her, but instead of getting some alone time to talk, she had to endure multiple lectures from family members.

Raven, the Queen of Corvids, stood statue-still, casting a shadow over the bed where Juni sat. Anyone else would be intimidated. Juni was simply annoyed.

"Lincoln filled us in with what happened until he lost consciousness." Raven crossed her arms over her metal breastplate. "Somehow from then to the time he woke up, you bound your life to Bane's and managed to heal Lincoln's wounds. We have theories, but I'd like to hear your story."

Geez. Mom and Dad had just finished grilling her on this.

Instead of answering right away, Juni glanced at Lincoln. They hadn't had a single moment alone together yet. They hadn't really spoken to each other.

Yet, he stayed by her side and held her hand, silently supporting her.

"You've been busy," Juni muttered at Raven.

"You seem to have forgotten how much you mean to me," Raven said.

"When you act like this, it's easy to forget." Juni clamped her mouth shut and winced. She didn't really mean that. She was tired and wanted to be alone with Lincoln. Couldn't Raven interrogate her tomorrow?

Her sister narrowed her eyes at Juni. "I think you made some sort of deal with Bane to free Lincoln and used the hōju to heal him. How am I doing?"

Pretty bang on. "Seems like you have it all figured out already."

Lincoln turned to her, one of his hands slipping over her thigh to rest on her leg just above the knee.

"So it's true?" he asked. "You used the hōju on me?"

She shrugged, her face growing warm again. They hadn't talked much about their feelings for each other. No time. Juni wasn't typically an insecure person, but what if Lincoln didn't feel as strongly as her? She still would've saved him, of course, but anyone with two brain cells would realize the extent of her feelings.

"Juni." Lincoln gripped her hand.

She swallowed and straightened. "Neither Bane nor I have healing abilities. I had already tied my life to that monster to break the barrier, release my divinity and defeat Hikaru. Seemed rather silly to let you bleed out at that point."

She cringed at her own harsh words. To an outsider, she probably came across as flippant, or petulant, no better than an angsty teenager, but she didn't fool anyone in the room, especially not Lincoln.

"You shouldn't have done it. You shouldn't have done any of this," Lincoln said. "I'm not worth it."

He'd said these words to her before, and just like the last time, she ignored them.

"You two can bicker about this later," Raven said. "I need to know the specifics of the deal."

Juni ripped her gaze from Lincoln's once again and diligently answered the rest of her sister's questions. Ignoring the trained fighter sitting beside her became harder and harder though, and Juni released an audible sigh of relief when Raven finally left the room.

Only to realize she was now alone with Lincoln.

And he knew exactly how she felt about him.

## CHAPTER 5

"You call it an expiration date..."
(Dramatic pause)
"I call it a spoiler alert."

— JUNI'S DAD

J uni's mind reeled. So much had happened in the last few days. The world continued to turn without pause or consideration for her situation. And now everything slowed to a standstill, focusing on this moment.

And all she did was stare at the door and listen to her sister's footsteps fade upstairs.

"Juni." Lincoln's voice sounded a little lower and more gravelly than usual.

She turned to him, her heart caught in her throat,

and his proximity started doing all sorts of other weird things in her body.

Lincoln slid his hand along her cheek to cradle the side of her face. His callouses from hours upon hours of training scratched her skin, his dark gaze searched hers.

When she didn't say anything, he leaned in.

She froze and held her breath.

He hesitated.

They stared at each other awkwardly while her heart thundered in her chest and threatened to break free of her ribcage.

"What's wrong?" Lincoln asked.

Where should she start? "Everything has changed."

He tensed, his hands balling into fists. "Nothing has changed for me."

Of course not, he wasn't the one tied to the Lord of War's life.

"I know your circumstances are not the same, and I would do anything to rewind time," he continued. "And I will do anything and everything to see you free of Bane."

Her heart started doing weird things again.

"But have your feelings for me changed?" he asked.

A wide range of evasions and excuses popped into her head. She could weasel her way out of this awkward discussion about touchy feely emotions. But why? What would be the point besides ruining something that hadn't yet had the chance to start?

Lincoln waited. Quiet and patient, like he had for the last six years.

"No," she admitted. If anything, her feelings for Lincoln had deepened, intensified.

Lincoln smiled. Not a regular smile. *The* smile. The one that could light up a room and blind half the occupants. The one he only showed her.

"Then nothing has changed for us, Juni. I like you and you like me."

"It's not that simple." And she was certainly beyond simply *liking* him.

He shook his head. "It really is."

"But Bane could..."

"Bane could do a number of things." Lincoln licked his lips. "But not this."

He pulled her close, leaned down and pressed his lips to hers.

Whatever arguments she had ran out the door.

Lincoln had a way of kissing her—as if breathing held no consequences, as if he stopped time itself for them to have this moment, as if he'd never taste her lips again.

And every time it did her in. She swung her leg around to straddle him. He groaned and one hand slipped down her back to the top of her hip to hold her in place. The other moved around her head to tangle in her knotted hair.

His lips curled under her mouth, probably saving some sort of joke about her mass of curls for later.

In this moment, she didn't care. She didn't care about her blood-encrusted outfit, the state of her hair, the significance of her caomhnóir bond and certainly not about her need for oxygen. She simply needed to consume Lincoln, stamp the feel of his lips on her brain so she could relish the memory forever.

Her phone buzzed in her pocket. She ignored it, rocking her hips against Lincoln's growing erection instead.

He nipped at her lips, his hands sliding down so he cupped her butt and squeezed. His fingertips dug in, and he pressed her down into his groin, encouraging the motion of her hips.

Her phone vibrated again.

Lincoln ripped his mouth away, breathing hard. "Is that your phone or is this how fox shifters say they're happy to see someone?"

"Shh." She pressed her finger to his lips and continued to rock, rubbing herself on him and making her head spin.

He groaned and rested his forehead against hers, shutting his eyes and gripping her butt.

The phone stopped for a whole second before vibrating again.

Lincoln leaned back and caught her finger in his mouth. He dragged his teeth along the skin. "I think you should answer it."

"You want to stop?" She frowned. She couldn't stop her hips now if she tried.

"I want you to get rid of whomever is calling so we can continue." The heat in his gaze could melt diamonds.

She ground against him to make him groan some more before pulling her phone from her pocket. The caller ID said Danielle Duke.

She frowned again. Her friend didn't normally call on repeat. She rarely called at all, preferring to text or send a message.

After pressing the accept button, she held the phone to her ear. "Hey, Dani. What's wrong?"

"I need your help," Dani whispered into the phone, the hysteria clear to anyone who knew her. As one of the three besties in their trio, Juni knew Dani better than most. Her friend was supposed to be on a romantic getaway with her boyfriend, Quinn.

"What happened?" Juni asked.

"Quinn's dead, and they think I killed him."

# CHAPTER 6

"What do you call it when a chickpea gets murdered?"
(Dramatic pause)
"Hummuside."

— JUNI'S DAD

L ong, lean, with smooth dark skin, piercing green eyes and naturally curly hair that never seemed to tangle like Juni's, Dani Duke had inspired a lot of jealousy in high school. After Dani punched Vance Monroe for trying to resurrect "Kick a Ginger Day" with Juni, she'd inspired a deep, life-long admiration and friendship.

And right now, as she stood outside her childhood home, Dani inspired some deep-seated maternal instinct Juni didn't know she possessed. Juni studied

Dani's dishevelled state and shifting gaze and raced to her friend, pulling her in for a big hug.

Juni wasn't the hugging type.

No, that wasn't quite right.

Juni hugged her family all the time, but mostly because they'd conditioned her since infancy, and she had no choice.

Dani's jaguar scent curled around Juni and tickled her nose. Though foxes would consider the large cats a dangerous predator in nature, having grown up together, shifted together and run together, Dani's scent didn't trigger any of Juni's survival instincts. Instead, it sent familiar warmth through Juni's body.

Dani clung to Juni and sobbed into her shoulder, her tears soaking through the thin fabric of her tee. Thankfully, Juni wore a clean shirt, having paused long enough to change from the blood-encrusted outfit.

Behind them, the sound of the car door closing broke the tearful reunion. Lincoln walked up the path to Dani's parents' place.

Dani broke away from Juni and scowled over her shoulder. "What's he doing here?"

Juni bit back a smile. Dani didn't like Lincoln. Not since high school when he'd broken Juni's heart and betrayed her. Juni might've forgiven Lincoln a long time ago, but it would take a lot longer and a lot more for her bestie to do the same.

"Good to see you again, Danielle," Lincoln said. Shoulders tense, gaze wary, he knew he approached a dangerous shifter who hated his guts. But he walked over to join them anyway.

"As if this day couldn't get any worse." Dani jerked her chin in Lincoln's direction. "Why did you bring him?"

"Uh..."

Dani narrowed her eyes at her. "Please tell me you're not giving this ding-dong a second chance."

Juni pulled at the collar of her shirt. Her clothing felt a little too tight all of a sudden. "Er..."

Trust Dani to push her own situation to the side to focus on her friend.

"A lot of things have changed," Juni said. Odin's sack of nuts, that sounded lame, even to her.

Dani snorted before jabbing her finger in the air at Lincoln. Her green eyes flashed yellow, showing the predator lurking beneath her skin. "If you hurt her again, I'll castrate you myself."

"If I hurt her again, I'll deserve much more than that." Lincoln shoved his hands in his pockets. "Maybe we should go in? As much as I love discussing my possible castration on the sidewalk, Juni nearly crashed three times getting here. Let's go inside, and you can tell us what happened. We came to help."

"We? Us?" Dani turned to Juni and jerked her thumb at Lincoln. "You do realize his mom got charged with littering every time she dropped him off at school, right?"

Juni chuckled and shook her head. "He has a point, Dani. You look like a before picture right now."

Her friend gasped, her hand going to her chest in fake outrage. That was the thing about growing up naturally blessed in the genetics department. Having a bad day was no big deal. Even in her current state, Dani was striking and could stop traffic.

"Fine." Dani dropped her hand, her expression growing serious again. "Let's go inside."

No one spoke as Dani led them up the creaking wood stairs and into the rectangular, split-level house with cedar plank siding. The house's familiar scent wrapped around Juni.

Dani's family had spaghetti last night, the tomato, basil and beef scents clinging to the air. The perfume Dani's mom preferred, and the tang of her dad's favourite beer also added to the bouquet. But all those smells didn't compare to the grief.

Tears and tissues.

The smell of sadness slammed into Juni like a wall, and she stumbled into the living room after Dani.

Her friend waved at the couches, but instead of making herself comfortable, Juni paced across the room while Lincoln leaned against the faded floral wallpaper. Dani gave them a one-shoulder shrug and flopped onto the couch. She reached over, grabbed a throw pillow and hugged it to her chest.

"Okay," Juni said. "Let's start at the beginning. I

know you and Quinn were having problems, but you planned a trip to the Okanagan. What happened?"

"We got in a fight. Like we always do." Dani lifted her head from the pillow. "He stalked out of the cabin and went for a walk."

"Where'd he go?"

"No idea. The cabin we rented was in the middle of an apple orchard in a fairly secluded location. There's nothing for miles."

"So he went on a walk to commune with nature... then what?"

"I waited for him, but he never returned. I fell asleep watching old reruns on television and the next thing I knew, it was morning, and the police were knocking at the door."

Dani's expression pinched, and she took a deep breath before continuing. "They came in, asked me if Quinn was staying with me. They'd apparently found his ID and called all the rentals in the area. Everything was going fine, sort of, until they found out I was a shifter."

"And then they arrested you," Juni guessed.

Dani nodded. "Apparently, the crime scene was... messy. They wouldn't let me see him. Even before they arrested me." Her bottom lip quivered, and she hugged the pillow tighter. "I didn't hear a thing."

Juni stopped pacing and flopped down on the cushion beside her friend. She reached out and wrapped her arm around Dani's shoulders and squeezed. "We'll find out what happened."

"I didn't do it."

"I know."

"You believe me?"

Juni withdrew her arm and tapped her nose. "You went straight from the holding cell to here after making bail and calling me. You haven't showered. I can smell your sweat and tears, but there's no blood on you. Not even under your nails, nor is there any heavy detergent or soap smell."

"Great Odin." Dani's eyes widened. "I knew your nose was good, but I had no idea it was that good."

Juni smiled, a little pain stabbing her chest. If only law enforcement and the courts recognized shifter-sourced evidence. Though society had made some steps toward equality, the Mortal Realm still very much operated on a system of tolerance, instead of acceptance. "I plan to use it to my advantage."

# CHAPTER 7

"What is the best part about working in a morgue?"
(Dramatic pause)
"Remains to be seen."

— JUNI'S DAD

Juni sat in the sauna-like interior of the vehicle as Lincoln pulled into a parking spot for the Okanagan hospital. The morgue stored the bodies of recently deceased people until someone identified and claimed them or until cremation or burial arrangements were made. In cases like Quinn's, the morgue also performed autopsies. From the little information she gleaned from the police over the phone, they didn't need the autopsy results to make a preliminary determination of the cause of death.

They still ordered it to do their due diligence and uncover any unknowns.

Lincoln shoved the gearshift into park but didn't move to get out of the vehicle. "Are you sure we should be here?"

He'd insisted on making the four-hour drive over the Coquihalla Highway with her. All this power and she still had to rely on mortal technology to get around. She might've unlocked her light fae powers, but she hadn't had a chance to practice portalling to unknown locations. She might never master that skill. Rourke, her sister's guardian, required a magical signal known as a key to portal to. Her necklace held such a key.

That's not what Lincoln had asked, though.

"Of course, we should be here," she said and frowned. "This is where the body is."

Lincoln leaned back in the driver's seat and took a deep breath. "That's not what I meant. Do you think it's a good idea for you, specifically you, to be here, when the Lord of War could snatch you at any time?"

Juni unsnapped her seatbelt and popped open the door. A wave of hot, sticky air swooshed into the vehicle.

Odin's nuggets. How could it possibly be hotter outside?

"Bane could *snatch* me no matter where I am, so being here..." She pointed at the car seat. "Instead of there." She jerked her thumb behind her back. "Makes no difference."

Lincoln picked up his phone from the centre console and shoved it in his pocket before he opened his own door.

"And before you suggest that I send one of my siblings, I'll stop you right there. They're already working on another case."

"You should all be working on getting rid of Bane," Lincoln muttered.

She narrowed her eyes at him. She didn't disagree, but aside from scouring the internet for information, which Mike programmed a bot to do, they didn't have any idea where to start or what to do. The Bane problem wouldn't solve itself overnight. It would take time and careful plotting.

Time being the key word.

Juni had never been the type of person to sit around, twiddling her thumbs, and waiting for something to happen. "I will not sit back and watch my friend go to jail for a crime she didn't commit."

Lincoln grumbled and hopped out of the car. "You know its's only a matter of time before they sic Rourke on us, right?"

Crap. He had a point. Though she adored the weapon-warper, his constantly unimpressed expression would be a mood killer for what she had planned later with Lincoln.

Juni stepped away from the car, and Lincoln locked it. "He'll give us alone time."

"That's not what I'm concerned about." He walked

around the car to join Juni. He reached out and entwined his hand with hers. He hadn't stopped touching her in some way since they'd retrieved her from Bane's cabin, as if he needed to reassure himself she was actually right there beside him.

"I just want you safe," Lincoln said.

She squeezed his hand, something that was quickly becoming a thing they did to comfort one another. "I am safe. I have you."

Lincoln looked away but not in time to hide the flinch. The tell drove an invisible knife through her heart. When Hikaru had laid a trap for her, Lincoln had ended up caught in the spell with only a dagger to fight the light fae kitsune warrior.

Lincoln hadn't hesitated.

To give Juni time to escape, he'd launched himself at Hikaru, knowing he'd likely die. The odds had been stacked against him. Despite intense training, Lincoln had lost that fight, almost paying for it with his life, but his sacrifice paid off. Juni had time to figure a way out of the situation. He'd saved them both.

Lincoln wouldn't see it that way, though.

She knew him well enough to see the emotions he tried so hard to hide. Her sister and brother-in-law had tasked him with her protection, and he'd done a spectacular job until that night. He felt like a failure. More specifically, he felt like he failed her.

Total nonsense, of course.

It would take time and patience for Lincoln to forgive himself, but she'd be there with him.

"So, you're just going to walk up to the counter and ask to sniff the corpse?" Lincoln held the door open for her, and they walked into the overly air-conditioned atmosphere. The cold air rushed over her skin.

Juni despised hospitals and generally tried to avoid them as a rule. The smells of...everything...bombarded her—patients' ailments and conditions, blood, tears, feces, semen, vomit. All the stuff.

When she was younger, it had been overwhelming. Now, though still unpleasant, she compartmentalized, resulting in a headache that made her cranky.

The coroner's office took everything the hospital provided in the smell department to the next level.

"Are you okay?" Lincoln studied her face, no doubt reading her like a book.

"Peachy."

"You don't look peachy. You look more like a ghost."

"Interesting choice of words." Their flip flops slapped the smooth flooring as they made their way to the morgue. Juni had never been here before, but it couldn't be that different from all the other hospitals because, so far, this one looked like the rest. Cool tones and shiny floors.

Juni tried not to think about what the morgue would smell like. Lincoln pushed the swinging door and held it open for her. She brushed past and wished she could dig her nose into his clothes and inhale him instead of this place.

Without hesitating, she walked to the front desk. An older woman with gray hair pulled into a bun looked up from a clipboard in front of her. She wore dark-rimmed glasses and had deep circles under her eyes. Her olive skin and almond-shaped eyes hinted at Mediterranean ancestry. Instead of providing one of those megawatt customer service smiles, she twitched when they approached, her mouth tightening, her eyes narrowing.

Juni pulled out her identification and held it away from her body for the woman to read. "My name is Juniper Crawford. I'm a private investigator with Crawford Investigations. I'd like to speak to the coroner, please."

The woman sighed and pushed her glasses back on her nose. Her scent coiled around her, but the fuzzy edge made Juni perk up. The woman was a shifter, but she couldn't place what kind. "That would be me. I'm Dr. Hasapi."

Juni straightened and smiled. "This might sound a little weird, but I'd like to sniff a body that was recently sent in for an autopsy."

"You're a shifter?" the coroner asked.

Juni nodded. "Fox."

"Which body?"

"Quinn George."

Dr. Hasapi narrowed her eyes and leaned forward. "The murder victim?"

Juni cleared her throat. "Yes."

This was the moment the coroner would most likely tell her no and possibly call security. That's why Juni came in person. Human nature made it difficult for regs and shifters alike to decline a request in person. Especially if the person was respectful and good natured and had a nice smile.

Maybe she should've had Lincoln ask. He could bat those beautifully long eyelashes at anyone and make them swoon.

"Just a sniff?" the coroner asked.

Juni nodded. "It doesn't break any rules and the information I pick up will help my investigation immensely without compromising the case." Shifter evidence was inadmissible in court, so the coroner wouldn't have to worry about the cops finding out the coroner let Juni in because Juni wouldn't end up in court testifying.

Dr. Hasapi hesitated, her head shaking back and forth a little as if she prepared to say no.

"I'm not asking for you to release your findings or share information that you discovered during the course of the autopsy. I just need to stand close to the body."

The coroner grumbled, but the fuzzy scent wafting from behind the desk bolstered Juni's confidence.

"They arrested a shifter for the crime," Juni added.

"Because they're a shifter?" The coroner narrowed her eyes.

Juni nodded.

"Jaguar?"

Juni nodded again and swallowed. The coroner only could've arrived at that conclusion one way.

"Her scent is all over the body," Dr. Hasapi said.

And there it was. Juni had expected it. Dani and Quinn were in a relationship and staying in a cabin together. Of course, her scent was all over the victim.

And Juni already knew Dani didn't kill her boyfriend. If she had, she wouldn't have asked Juni for help to clear her name. She wouldn't have waited meekly in the cabin for the police to arrive and arrest her. She'd have disposed of the body and called if she needed help covering it up.

"The jaguar didn't commit the crime. The wounds were not consistent with claw marks or bites from long canines." The coroner stood and walked around the desk. "I'll show you."

"What or who do you think caused Quinn's death?" Lincoln asked.

Technically, the coroner didn't have to answer. She shouldn't answer. This was an active investigation after all. The coroner pushed open a swinging door and waved for them to enter ahead of her. "I'm not sure. I've never seen anything like this before. I'll let you see for yourself."

Dr. Hasapi walked over to a row of cadaver drawers. They probably had a proper name, but Juni's name fit them better.

"Brace yourself." The coroner pulled a drawer out from the second row. Frigid air rushed from the refrigerated unit along with the smell of death.

Contrary to common belief, morgues themselves weren't smelly—at least not to a reg nose. The refrigeration of bodies between two and four degrees Celsius slowed the rate of decay, because the microbes that broke down the tissue found it more difficult to flourish in colder temperatures. The good news for Juni and her nose, the microbes were also the culprits for producing most of the bad smells in a decaying corpse. Less microbes, less decay and less stinky stuff. Less, but not non-existent.

The room had an antiseptic smell to regs like Lincoln, but to Juni, a fox shifter with a sense of smell on steroids, things were different.

She not only smelled the death and the start of decay on the body of her bestie's dead boyfriend, but the bodies in the other drawers as well.

Nothing was one hundred percent sealed, and Juni smelled it all.

"Not so bad." Lincoln's normally tanned skin paled.

Juni wasn't an idiot. Lincoln had killed before. For her. He'd turned into a killer. For her. But he probably didn't stick around to study the dead bodies.

She patted his arm while her nose tried to curl

away from the smell. She had seen more than her fair share of cadavers—an unpleasant reality of her job—but never someone she'd known.

Up until now, she'd focused on helping her friend and had purposefully not thought about Quinn—not out of disrespect but self-preservation.

Quinn and Dani had a tumultuous relationship. They fought about pretty much everything. Their constant bickering had become a backdrop to social events. But in all that conflict, Quinn had always respected Dani and her friends. He wasn't the bad guy in this story. He wasn't physically or emotionally abusive. He never called Dani names. He wasn't a narcissist. He was a great guy who had opposing beliefs with the woman he loved, and desperately tried to find a way to make it work despite them growing apart more and more each day.

Juni had asked Dani once why they stayed together when they fought all the time. She'd simply replied that it was hard to let go of the person you loved. She wasn't ready yet.

Now, looking down at the man who'd been in her friend's life for years, Juni felt empty, hollow. As though her stomach dropped and disappeared.

Lincoln placed a hand on her shoulder, a question in his gaze.

How attuned he must be to her to sense the change in her emotions. She hadn't said a thing. Her eyes watered, threatening to spill, and she blinked the tears back.

Time to focus. Her emotions needed to sit on the sidelines for the moment.

Juni leaned forward, bending a little at the waist to examine Quinn. Or what was left of him.

Though most of his body lay in a mangled heap on the slab, his head remained intact, his high cheekbones, slightly hooked nose, full lips and light brown skin a familiar sight. His face, though slack, tugged on memories that Juni couldn't afford to let spiral up.

His closed eyelids hid his expressive brown eyes and made him appear at peace. And wherever he was, Juni hoped that was true.

Taking in a deep breath, Juni sampled the air. The first inhale made her nose curl again for exactly the same reason, but after the initial shock of Quinn's scent mixed with death and terror passed, something else rose up.

That couldn't be right.

She sniffed again.

Nope. Definitely still there.

She looked up and met the coroner's gaze. "Elk? A deer of some sort?"

"Moose." Ah. That explained it. As a resident of the Lower Mainland, she ran in the local forests and had come across a number of non-supernatural wildlife, but nothing like this.

Wait. "Moose? Are you sure?"

The coroner nodded, and they all looked down at the mauled body.

"A moose killed Quinn?"

"I'm not sure if the moose was responsible for the death. It might be that the moose found the deceased post mortem..."

And decided to trample it? What in the Underworld...

"...And the dead body spooked it."

Juni squeezed her eyes shut. "Will that be in your official report to the police?"

The coroner nodded. "There's enough moose hair present that I can include it in my findings, but I can't include any of the information I obtained using my shifter senses."

"Of course not." They'd throw out the report if the coroner did that because that was the level of distrust between the reg and shifter communities.

"So..." Lincoln cut in. "Can someone fill in the non-shifter in the room?" he asked, still pale and making a concerted effort not to look at the body in front of him.

"There's only Dani's and the moose's scent on the body," Juni said. "The wounds are not consistent with a jaguar's teeth or claws, and jaguars typically deliver kill shots to the back of the head, so even the placement and extent of the wounds doesn't fit. I've never heard of a moose mauling anyone, and the animal's hair present on the body will not be convincing enough to free Dani automatically."

"Enough to create doubt for a jury?" Lincoln sounded hopeful.

Juni snorted. "If the jury was balanced with regs and non-regs, maybe. We don't want this to go to court."

"Moose attacks do occur, but it's rare and I've never seen one like this." Dr. Hasapi bobbed her head. "They'll claim the moose wounds were delivered afterward, all a part of the shifter's master plan to cover up the murder. They will also argue the partner had motive and means."

"That's lame," Lincoln said.

"That's what it's like to be a shifter," the coroner huffed. "I concealed what I was for the majority of my career."

They stood silently around the dead body, each in their own thoughts. She couldn't read Lincoln's mind, but he looked like he wanted to break something.

Juni turned to the coroner. "Thank you for your assistance."

"I hope everything works out." Her tone implied she didn't like Dani's odds, but Juni still had a plan.

And hope.

As she pushed through the doors to the heat outside, she turned to Lincoln. "Looks like we're going moose hunting."

"Is that so?" Rourke stepped out of nowhere.

# CHAPTER 8

"Why wouldn't the librarian tell me where to find the
self-help section?"
(Dramatic pause)
"She said it would defeat the purpose."

— JUNI'S DAD

Juni stood on the landing of the hospital's
entrance and tried not to look guilty. Faced
with the rage playing across the face of the
weapon-warping dark fae warrior standing
across from her, she failed. Miserably.

"You look off," Rourke said.

Out of everyone in her sister's court, aside from her
sister and Lincoln, Rourke knew her best. They'd spent
a lot of time over the years training. After getting

abducted by a pack of hyena shifters, Juni had felt vulnerable and weak, and Rourke had taught her how to use that fear to become a fighter.

"I have a case," she said.

"A case?" Both of Rourke's eyebrows shot up. "Do you really think now is a good time to run around catching cheating spouses and fraudsters?"

She folded her arms over her chest. "Dani has been arrested for murder."

Rourke stopped scowling. "We'll break her out and take her to your sister's court."

"It doesn't work—" She pinched the bridge of her nose. "She didn't do it."

"I don't care," Rourke said. "If any of us were bound by human law, we'd also be in jail."

Lincoln grunted. As the one reg in the conversation, he was arguably bound by human law. Shifters, too, but Juni could always apply for political asylum with her sister's court.

Rourke shrugged. "Your system is a little broken."

Now that was laughable.

Rourke's system of choice would maim and kill.

"Well, you can put away your jail-breaking skills," she said. "Dani is out on bail and her parents put forth the bond, so they'll all be pissed if you ran off with her now."

"You have the funds to correct that," Rourke pointed out.

Now it was Juni's turn to scowl. Raven had set up

the entire family for financial independence when she became the Queen of Corvids. The title came with a room full of gold, and a target on her back. Raven wanted to ensure the family was set if something happened to her.

Juni hadn't touched it. For some reason, she couldn't bring herself to spend the money.

No. That was a lie. She knew precisely why she wanted nothing to do with the funds. It was blood money. Her sister paid for it with her life. Raven might still be alive, but the only way off the throne was if someone else with corvid essence killed her.

If Juni spent the money...

She shivered. "That's not an option."

"Mortals are so weird," Rourke said.

"I'm not a mortal. I'm a light fae shifter. A perfectly capable one, by the way. We don't need a babysitter."

Shadows covered Lincoln's face, but he blanked his expression when she raised her eyebrow at him.

"Well, I can't let you lovebirds have all the fun." Rourke folded his arms over his leather fae armour.

"You can't stop Bane from taking me if he shows up," she said.

Lincoln shifted on his feet. He better not try to stop Bane if he showed up, but his stubborn expression said he would.

"It's not Bane I'm worried about," Rourke said.

Juni waited.

Lincoln spoke up. "It's Bane's enemies."

Her stomach lurched. She hadn't thought of that. Lincoln had, but she hadn't. She smacked her forehead with her palm and dragged her fingers down her face. Ugh! Why was she such an idiot? Of course, she had more than Bane to worry about. If his horde of enemies discovered he had a guardian—a weak, newly-fledged, light fae, fox shifting guardian—they'd relish the opportunity to hurt the Lord of War.

"I'm guessing because Bane's a giant turd, he's got more than a few enemies." Lincoln looked at Rourke for confirmation.

Rourke didn't even bother responding, the answer was obviously yes.

Great. Like Juni needed more things to worry about.

"Come on." She waved at her car parked on the side of the road. "Let's go track a moose."

Rourke blinked. "A what?"

Lincoln clapped him on the back. "We'll fill you in on the drive."

# CHAPTER 9

"My deer-cloning business is now accepting
applications."
(Dramatic pause)
"It's a great way to make a quick buck."

— JUNI'S DAD

Back at the cabin, Juni trotted out of the
bedroom in fox form and let the sensory information engulf her. In human form, she had
heightened senses far superior to that of a reg, but in
fox form everything intensified.

Rourke and Lincoln froze in the living room, their
eyes wide.

She stopped in her tracks. What happened? Why

were they both looking at her like that? They'd both seen her in fox form before. She looked like a prettier version of a Shiba Inu.

"Uh...Juni..." Lincoln ran his hand through his thick black hair.

She cocked her head.

Rourke and Lincoln exchanged a look before Lincoln walked over and picked her up.

This close to him, his scent curled around her, warm and familiar, like a blanket. His heart beat steadily, and his arms wrapped around her. She could stay like this forever.

Lincoln walked her into the bathroom and turned her to face the mirror.

Why was he frowning so ha—

Odin's shriveled nuggets.

She snarled at her reflection. Instead of her normal orange fur, her fox form had turned completely white.

She flicked her tail in anger and froze again.

What in the everlasting fuck was that?

She had two tails. She swished them again and growled.

Lincoln readjusted her in his arms so he could run his hand down her back.

Was he petting her like a dog?

He continued to stroke her.

Did he honestly think that would calm her down right—

*Oh.*

*Oh, that was nice.*

*Wait.*

*No.*

She shook her coat, and Lincoln dropped his face to her fur, inhaling her scent deeply.

Letting her anger go, she relaxed in Lincoln's arms. She could freak out about the colour change, additional tail and what it all meant later.

With a wiggle, Lincoln got the message and gently set her on the ground.

When she walked back into the living room, Rourke stood where she'd left him.

"Your brother's fox is also white, if that makes it any easier," Rourke said.

Oddly, it did. If only she'd been around to witness Mike's cursing and tantrum.

She flashed her teeth at Rourke. She also wagged her tails, but it felt so weird she stopped. Time to focus, anyway. She sniffed the ground.

No blood. Just as she expected.

Quinn had left the cabin hale and hearty. After sniffing around a bit more to ensure she processed the scene correctly, she pawed the door and waited for Lincoln to open it before dashing off.

"Hey!" Lincoln called out.

She yipped, and the men collectively groaned somewhere behind her before they began jogging to keep up.

Following Quinn's trail was easy. He'd stomped off to the orchard, leaving anger in his wake to cling to the leaves and dead grass.

"Running in this heat is less than ideal," Rourke grumbled. "I think she's trying to kill us."

"Story of my life," Lincoln answered.

They were a sight to behold. Both tall, strong and covered with weapons, the two warriors moved at an easy pace despite their grumbling. They hadn't broken a sweat yet.

The air turned sour, and Juni stopped to snort and shake her head.

Ugh.

Rotting apples. The orchard was littered with them. Juni tried to sniff the ground again, but the sharp smell of the fermenting fruit stabbed at her nose.

She snorted again and tried to catch the scent.

No luck.

She whined and pawed the ground. Thankfully, she didn't rely solely on her nose. Time to follow the trampled grass.

Juni didn't take long to find the crime scene. Quinn had died under the stars in the middle of an apple orchard, too far from the cabin for his lover to hear his screams.

The blood-stained soil and grass had been turned up by shoes and hooves. Jagged divots in the dirt made a path as well, like fingertips dug into the ground.

Quinn had tried to drag himself away.

Her hackles raised at the same time an invisible weight dropped in her belly. His death hadn't been fast. Or peaceful. It had been violent, and Quinn's terror still flavoured the air.

"Poor guy," Rourke muttered.

Neither man needed fox senses to follow the horrific attack.

The hoof prints trampling the area confirmed the other scent on Quinn's body. A moose very clearly mauled Quinn to death. Other than the reg scents littering the crime scene post-mortem, no one else had been here.

Just the moose and Quinn.

Moose shifter?

Had to be.

What else would explain this? Juni had never heard of a moose attack before, and the coroner said those were rare. A moose shifter made more sense, but why would a shifter target Quinn?

She turned away from the blood-soaked soil and followed the large hoof prints clambering away from the orchard.

Moose could be found in almost all Canadian forests from the Alaskan border to the eastern tip of Newfoundland and Labrador. With five hundred thousand to a million moose in Canada, seeing hoof prints wasn't out of the ordinary. Though Juni rarely saw moose, she'd always liked them. They were powerful swimmers, could dive underwater for food, had incredibly poor eyesight and were so ugly, they were endearingly cute.

Except this one.

This one most likely killed Quinn.

The trail led to a river and disappeared from there. The moose must've travelled either up or down the babbling water. This had to be a moose shifter, using the river to hide their trail.

What had Quinn done to cause a shifter to attack after him so brutally?

She snarled at the water as it rushed by.

"Do I even want to know what's going on?" A familiar voice broke through the sounds of nature.

Juni whipped around in time to watch Bane step from his portal of horrors. Rourke and Lincoln moved to block her with their bodies.

Bane's arrival had not surprised them. They always had her back.

Bane gave Lincoln a scathing look—up and down, before turning away dismissively. Annoyance pinged along their bond.

His reaction to Rourke was much more interesting, and confusing. She received a spattering of emotions—surprise, anger, and hurt.

Hurt?

Before she could probe the bond for more information, he clamped down on his feelings and all she got was ice.

Fine then.

"A fae, a reg, and a shifter were alone in the forest." Bane peered around Rourke's hulking body to pin her with his dark gaze. "There's a joke in there somewhere."

He was the joke, but she didn't have a human mouth to snap back at him. Instead, she sent irritation through their bond, but it hit the emotional blockade he'd built.

Bane smirked and turned to Lincoln. "I guess the punchline must be you." He jerked his chin in Rourke's direction. "How does it feel to be the second choice?"

Juni snarled.

Lincoln flicked his wrist, and a dagger appeared in his hand. "I don't care if I'm her second, twentieth, or one-hundredth choice. As long as she picks me in the end."

*Oh, swoon.*

Bane rocked back on his heels. "Fucking senti-mental regs."

"Did you come here to irritate us?" Rourke asked, a dagger magically appearing in his hand, too. "Because you've succeeded. Congratulations. You can leave now."

"I came to retrieve my guardian."

"No," Lincoln said.

"You can't keep her from me, boy."

"We're aware." Lincoln's tone was dry. "But she's

investigating a murder her best friend has been arrested for. If you take her now, she'll never forgive you."

"She already hates me," Bane said. "How much worse can it get?"

Both Lincoln and Rourke remained silent. She couldn't see their expressions, but she could imagine their identical flat stares. She'd been on the receiving end from both of them enough times.

If she'd been in human form, she would've laughed her ass off. As a fox, she hacked.

Bane responded with his typical scowl, or rather, a deepening of his already existing scowl.

"Fine," he said.

Without another word, he threw down a lodestone and stepped into the red haze. When the portal closed, Juni released a long breath. Bane's last look hadn't been directed at her.

She turned to Rourke, but Lincoln beat her to the question.

"What's up with you two?" Lincoln asked.

Rourke's expressive face warped into an indifferent mask, and the dagger in his hand disappeared into one of the many hidden sheaths on his person. "Too much to get into now."

Lincoln also sheathed his weapon and turned to her. "What's the plan?"

She examined the riverbank and the setting sun.

Although she'd evade most nocturnal predators, even in an unfamiliar landscape, and knew the men would protect her, picking up the moose's trail in the morning would be easier. And she was exhausted.

With a huff, she trotted back toward the cabin.

"Looks like we're calling it a night," Rourke said.

## CHAPTER 10

"Thieves broke into the grocery store last night."
(Dramatic pause)
"They got arrested for disturbing the peas."

— JUNI'S DAD

J uni sat on the bed in the guest room of her sister's Corvid Court fortress across from Rourke and Lincoln. She hadn't thought the investigation this far ahead. After returning to the cabin to retrieve her clothes, they'd spent hours trying to find accommodations for the night. Finally, Lincoln suggested leaving her choker in the car and using a lodestone to travel to the Shadow Realm. Tomorrow, they'd portal back to her necklace, which contained the location key.

Juni could've also gone home, but she had no plans to entertain another lecture from her parents. Her phone had pinged all day, alternating with texts from Dad with his terrible dad jokes, and ones from Mom telling her to remember to use protection. They'd get worse if she went home.

Instead, she had to watch Rourke and Lincoln's mental battle.

"Are you two about done?" she asked.

"With what?" Rourke responded without looking away from Lincoln.

"The staring contest." She waved at them, but the motion was completely wasted. Neither looked over to see it.

"I'm just waiting for Lincoln to agree that I'm right," Rourke said.

Juni sighed and flopped back on the bed. That would never happen, at least not when it concerned her.

"You cannot be left alone," Rourke continued.

"We're in my sister's court," she pointed out.

"Which assassins have infiltrated before," Rourke said.

"And lost," she said.

"They lost because either I, Cole or Raven killed those that got past all the other security measures."

"Exactly. I'm capable of defending myself." She sat up and folded her arms.

Rourke's expression softened. "Juni..."

"Even your sister, the Queen of Corvids is rarely left on her own," Lincoln finally said. "It's not a weakness to accept help."

Whose side was he on?

"I didn't say I was refusing help. I said I didn't want you both standing over the bed while I slept because that's creepy."

Rourke blinked at her as if she spoke utter nonsense. How many times had he had to stand guard while her sister slept?

Her stomach twisted. Odin's left nut. Would she have to watch over Bane like that?

The lingering taste from their take-out dinner turned sour in her mouth.

"Fine," she said. "Lincoln stays." She pointed at Rourke. "But you will have to guard from outside."

Something flashed across Rourke's face too fast for her to register before he turned to Lincoln. "Try to stay vigilant."

Lincoln nodded, and Rourke left the room, shutting the door behind him with a soft click. Lincoln's triumphant expression turned serious. He stood from his seat and stalked across the room.

Uh-oh.

He bent low enough to place one knee beside her and weave his hand through her hair to grip the back of her neck.

"Finally," he said.

He pressed his mouth to hers. This wasn't a sweet

kiss, or a tame one. This kiss spoke of longing and need, and she was one hundred percent here for it. His tongue stroked her own and sent fire racing through her veins.

She tugged him down and fell back onto the soft quilt. She needed to feel more of Lincoln—not just to slake the ache intensifying within her, but also to reassure herself that he was real. She hadn't dreamt it.

He'd almost died, and that scared the crap out of her.

She hadn't had the time to process any of it, but along with all the other feelings rushing to the surface, the fear came, too. She'd almost lost him.

She pulled him closer, clinging to his hard body. Inari had healed Lincoln, and he was alive and remaking her world with each flick of his tongue.

He pulled back, maybe to look at her, maybe to catch his breath. His gaze wild, he studied her, emotions flickering across his face.

"How'd you become such a great kisser?" she asked.

His grin wiped away the serious expression. "My mom always gave me those things from the electric mixer when she was baking."

"The ones covered with icing?"

He winked.

"You must have quite the sweet tooth."

"Mmmm..." He ducked his head but this time,

instead of kissing her lips again, he explored her jaw, then her ear, then her neck.

Her fingertips tingled, her claws threatening to come out as pleasure rolled through her body. She gripped the quilt underneath her with both hands. She'd fooled around with guys before but never anyone who meant as much to her as Lincoln did. And she never let it get too far.

Already, Lincoln made her skin sing, her body ache. She wanted to feel his weight on her, his skin sliding along hers. Something else thrummed in her blood and throbbed inside of her. Magic. Light fae power wound around Lincoln, pressing into his body to stroke and play.

Lincoln gasped and leapt off the bed. With two daggers appearing in his hands, he scanned the room. He didn't have any magic of his own, but the way he handled his weapons, he definitely gave the impression he wielded some sort of invisible power.

Cool air fanned her body where he'd hovered.

"What in the Underworld was that?" Lincoln's eyes widened.

She sat up and peered around the room. Had Lincoln lost his mind? What was he talking about? She raised an eyebrow and tried very hard not to notice Lincoln's massive erection.

And failed.

"Eyes up here, Crawford." He pointed at his face. "Did you feel that?"

She licked her lips. "I felt a lot of things. You'll have to be more specific."

He flashed her a wicked grin that made all sorts of promises before he turned serious again. "The magic. I felt it."

Juni froze. She ran through the moments leading up to Lincoln flying off the bed. She'd felt magic release from her body. When she fought Hikaru, she'd accessed her light fae power, but since then, she hadn't had time to explore her new power. Akin to willing the change, she'd consciously controlled her power. It came naturally to her, but this magic had a different flavour and effect.

"I think that was me," she said.

Lincoln sat on the corner of the bed and reached over to cover her hand with his.

"What did it feel like?" she asked.

"Exquisite."

She pushed his shoulder with her free hand.

"No. Seriously. I've never felt anything like it before, but I want you to do it again." His gaze flashed. "Now that I know it came from you. I want you to cover me with it."

"Pervert."

He nodded emphatically. "Absolutely."

Closing her eyes, she reached within and found the well of light she'd sensed earlier. There, in her chest, behind her sternum, magic pulsed, welcoming. Almost as if the power had a mind of its own and wanted her to know how excited it was to see her, the light fae essence pulsed the moment she focused on it.

Grasping the power, she sent tendrils of magic to caress Lincoln's face.

He shivered.

"Good? Bad?"

"Definitely good."

"What's it like?"

He shrugged, his eyes closing to half slits. If he were a cat shifter, he'd probably purr right now.

"It's hard to explain," he said. "I remember something similar when I woke up in that cave. It must've been Inari's magic, but this is all you."

"You can tell?"

"I..." He paused and cocked his head. "It's like it's sending me a message of what you're feeling. Like emotional feedback."

She frowned. That made no sense. How would sending Lincoln her feelings be useful anyway? How would that have helped her defeat Hikaru?

"Keep doing what you're doing with your magic. I want to try something." Lincoln leaned forward and ran his finger down her face. He made a lazy path along her neck, following the contour of her breast before coming to a stop at her nipple. Even through her clothing, the heat of his touch sent shivers of anticipation racing through her body.

He shuddered. "I feel all of that."

"Of course, you do. It's your finger on my boob, dummy."

"True." He winked and squeezed her breast playfully. "But your magic is telling me how much you like it."

Juni groaned. "Just my luck. I get saddled with useless magic that helps other people get off."

Lincoln's gaze danced. "I can help make things even."

She snorted but didn't dodge him when he leaned in again.

The air buzzed with more magic. But this time not hers.

Lincoln roughly shoved her to the bed, smothered her with his body and flung out his arm at the same time a fae stepped from a glittering portal. Two daggers protruded from the would-be assassin's chest. The woman, who looked no older than Juni, widened her eyes before toppling over. Her dark hair spilled around her as a pool of blood spread from her body.

Juni lay frozen under Lincoln's body. The air rasped through her lungs as she drew in air and tried to calm her nerves.

An assassin had tried to kill her.

Juni shoved Lincoln off her, and they both leapt from the bed to get a closer look at the body. Everything happened so fast.

"How'd she portal into this area of the fortress?"

Lincoln didn't speak at first. He clenched two new daggers in his hands and glared at the assassin.

Juni rested her hand on his arm, and he jerked back as if she woke him from a dream. Or a nightmare.

"It's okay. She's already dead. Your stare won't kill her."

"It's not okay," he growled. "I got distracted. What if she came five minutes later?"

She raised her eyebrows. "Five minutes, huh? Is that all you think it'll take?"

He turned to her, his gaze still wild and full of promise. "I will take all the time I need." He stepped closer. "Until I erase any thoughts of other people getting off on your magic."

"I wasn't planning on using my magic as a party trick." She flung her hands up. "There's only you."

He grumbled and looked away.

"Shouldn't we get someone to take care of her?"

"I'm not leaving you."

No, he wouldn't leave her side, that was clear from the set of his jaw and the tension in his shoulders, but any hope of continuing where they left off went out the window. Or rather, bleeding out with the assassin.

She needed to find more secure accommodations. Surveying her room, she mentally said goodbye. She'd stayed here countless times and never thought to be concerned for her safety. Raven took home security to the next level. This assassin had either been well-connected, financially backed or working with someone from the inside to get a lodestone to open to this room through all of Raven's shields.

Juni shivered.

Once Rourke discovered what happened, he'd make her move to another room, which was a shame, because she loved this bed.

Juni narrowed her eyes and examined the bed closer. "That dagger wasn't there before."

A long dagger was imbedded in the tufted headboard above where she'd been with Lincoln. Sunk at least two inches in, the blade had forced some of the stuffing out.

She spun around to Lincoln.

He shrugged, the action revealing ripped material. She closed the distance and pulled the leather back, sticky with blood, to examine the cut underneath,

"It's a scratch," Lincoln said.

Well, now. Lincoln had a way of under exaggerating his wounds.

The cut wasn't fatal, nor would it continue to bleed all over the place once he got stitches, but it wasn't exactly a scratch either.

"It needs stitches."

"It needs a couple of butterfly bandages. I'll be fine."

She grumbled but let go of the fabric. Sometimes she had to choose her battles, especially when dealing with the overprotective men in her life. Lincoln would live, regardless of how he tended to this wound, and that's all that mattered.

"Any chance of letting me kiss it better?" she asked.

"I'm onto you, temptress." Lincoln waggled his finger at her. "You will not distract me with your good looks and wicked tongue."

Rourke chose that moment to barge in. He looked at Juni, then Lincoln, then the dead body. His glower returned and settled on her.

She raised her hands again. "It's not my fault."

Rourke backed up enough to lean out the door and bark orders at some poor dark fae guard. They'd attempt to identify the assassin, but most likely, they wouldn't discover much. Assassins didn't tend to leave a trail.

"I don't care what you wish, princess. We're taking you to a more secure location for the night and you *will* have another guard in the room."

Lincoln leaned in and whispered, "Still want to make out?"

She shoved his shoulder, which only served to make him chuckle and Rourke's glower to darken.

Ugh.

Juni followed her sister's guardian from the room and resigned herself to uncomfortable sleep.

# CHAPTER 11

"What did the eagle say to the hunter?"
(Dramatic pause)
"It's ill-eagle to hunt."

— JUNI'S DAD

Juni scowled at the riverbed and kept walking. Large rocks lined the bank of the babbling river making their path difficult. The muggy, Okanagan air threatened to stifle them and even the shade of the coniferous trees offered little reprieve from the sweltering heat. Juni much preferred the more temperate climate of home.

Rourke cursed every ten steps or so.

"This would be faster if we spread out," she said.

"Not a chance," Lincoln said.

Rourke didn't bother to respond at all. He wouldn't let that happen, either. Especially not after the assassin's visit.

"The shifter could be anywhere by now," she complained and kicked a rock.

More silence. Now Lincoln wasn't even taking the bait.

Ugh.

She continued to walk along the river's edge on the bank opposite of where she lost the scent. If they didn't find the moose shifter soon, they might not be able to prove the moose was responsible for Quinn's death. Every minute that passed gave the shifter time to hide evidence and slip away.

"Have you thought about what you're going to do with the shifter when you find them?" Lincoln asked.

She stumbled on the rocks. No, she hadn't, but she wasn't about to admit it. "I thought we could beat them up and portal them to the police station."

"Do you have a lodestone for that location?" Rourke finally deigned to speak. "Or have you developed portalling abilities over night?"

Dang it.

"It was a good attempt," Lincoln said. "To try to cover up your lack of a plan."

She scowled at him, which only made his smile grow. His white teeth flashed under the sun, and his heated look made her stumble again on the uneven rocks.

"And what if it's an actual bonafide moose?" Rourke asked, kindly ignoring how she flailed on the bank of the river because Lincoln's beauty distracted her.

"It's not," she said.

"Humour me. What if it's an actual moose instead of a moose shifter? What then?" Rourke asked.

Why was he so Odin-loving bent on asking the hard questions? Did he not get enough coffee this morning?

"You can portal back to the fortress, grab some chains or rope and get Raven."

"She's a little busy at the moment," Rourke said.

"With what?" she asked. "The missing person's case?"

"That, too." Rourke frowned. "But right now, she's trying to find a way to release you from your bond with Bane."

She stumbled again. Of course, that's what Raven was doing. Her sister might try to hide it, but she was the biggest softy of them all. Raven loved the family fiercely and would do anything for any of them, including putting herself in danger.

"Fine," Juni said. "I'll get Bear."

Both men shook their heads.

Dang it. She didn't need to ask why they responded like that.

Her oldest brother, Raven's twin, must've gone off grid. Again.

"What's Cole up to?" Juni asked. Though her brother-in-law was lethal efficiency personified, he didn't scare Juni. Maybe he should. Maybe they'd all become desensitized to the brutality and trickery of the dark fae due to their constant exposure.

Rourke turned thoughtful. "I believe he's fuming about being left behind."

That fit. Cole would lock Raven up in a padded room if her sister let him. He had to be unaware of Raven's condition. If he knew, he'd never let her out of his sight.

"Okay. The plan is to find the moose. If it's a shifter, we capture it the good old-fashioned way. If it's an actual moose, we find Cole. Either way, we exonerate my friend." Easy.

"Hopefully before lunch." Lincoln's stomach growled as if on command.

She rolled her eyes and kept tramping along the river's edge, her senses open and searching for signs of a moose.

After another hour, she admitted defeat. "I don't think the moose came this way."

"So what now?" Lincoln asked.

"We cross the river and search the other side until we return to our starting location."

"And then we cross again and continue in the other direction?" Lincoln finished.

"Pretty much. Essentially, we'll make a figure eight with the moose's entry point at the middle."

Rourke grumbled something too quiet for even her fox hearing to pick up.

"What was that?" she asked.

"I was one of the top assassins in the guild. I'm the bonded guardian to the Queen of Corvids."

"And now you're babysitting her younger, immature sister," Juni finished for him. "I get it. So humiliating. Would it help if I ran into an enemy's camp and placed myself in harm's way needlessly?"

"Make sure you trip when you try to run away from them as well," Lincoln piped up.

Rourke smirked before his expression grew sullen again. "It's not that. And no, please don't do that. I don't think you need me to point out that you've already done something remarkably similar by running off to Bane to become his caomhnóir."

She ignored his point, too accurate for her liking. "So what's the problem?"

"I've literally become a moose hunter." His shoulders slumped forward, and his face pinched in as if he were in physical pain.

He looked so defeated.

Juni tried to bite back her laughter.

Rourke scowled, flashing his pointed teeth.

"You're really more of a moose hunter's assistant," Lincoln said. "At best."

If Rourke could murder with a glare, Lincoln would lay dead on the forest floor.

Juni opened her mouth to add to Rourke's torture, but a branch snapped, and they all stilled.

Juni raised her face and sniffed. She stood upwind from the source. Just her luck. She jerked her head in the direction of the sound, and the men followed her as she moved toward it.

Five dark fae stepped from the tree cover.

"Those aren't moose." Lincoln unsheathed both his daggers.

"What do you want?" Juni asked.

Their grim expressions answered for them.

"They're not here to talk, Juniper." Rourke stepped up beside her.

The fae lunged forward in a coordinated attack.

One warrior didn't have a chance to complete his first step before one of Rourke's daggers found his chest. The others moved fast enough to dodge.

Too fast.

Juni unsheathed her daggers and ducked out of the way of a fae warrior who'd broken past Lincoln and Rourke. The magic inside her sang, pushing against the invisible barrier. She released the power, letting it fuse with her essence and flow through her veins. The song bubbled out of her lips, and she sang as she spun away from the fae's attack. Faster and faster, she moved around the warrior, slashing and stabbing as the song consumed her.

The warrior screeched and covered his ears before crumpling to the ground.

Juni stopped moving, but the music still pulsed in her veins. She swayed to the sound of the light fae magic dancing within her. As the song faded, awareness of her surroundings crystalized and intensified.

She turned to find Rourke and Lincoln gaping at her. The other men lay bleeding on the ground at their feet. The daggers in Lincoln and Rourke's hands dripped with blood, but neither paid any attention.

"Were you...singing?" Rourke finally broke the silence.

She shrugged. "I was feeling it."

They both blinked at her.

Okay, even she realized how weird that sounded, but what else could she say? How else could she explain what had just happened? She told the truth.

Sort of.

Instead of making eye contact, or explaining further, she jerked her chin at the dead fae. "I take it you didn't have any problems taking these ones down?"

"Not after you sang them to death," Lincoln said.

"Good." Wait. "What?"

She rocked back on her heels. Clearly, she must've misheard him. "I'm not picking up what you're putting down."

Lincoln sighed and knelt by one of the warriors to wipe his daggers clean. "As pretty as your voice is..."

Rourke coughed and turned away.

She narrowed her eyes at the guardian's shaking

shoulders before returning her attention to Lincoln. "Go on."

"It's like your song made them forget all their training. One moment, I was fighting for my life, worried my skills might not match up, and the next, the warrior started hesitating and fumbling."

"Sloppy footwork and slow strikes," Rourke added. "To me, it seemed as though someone..." He gave her a pointed look. "Drained them of energy."

Well, crap. That wasn't such a bad skill to have, but if others found out, they might try to use her, or find some way to neutralize her skill. Bane would definitely be pleased to discover this information.

Odin's fried meat sack.

If Raven found out, she'd try to lock Juni away in some misguided attempt to protect her.

"Don't tell my sister," she pleaded.

Rourke's expression darkened. "I'll keep your secret for now, princess. But only by omission. If Raven asks, or if it becomes apparent the information is essential to convey, I will sing like a canary."

"Interesting choice of words," Lincoln muttered.

"That's my line." She spoke the words half-heartedly while she processed Rourke's comment. He was her sister's guardian, not hers. No matter how close they'd become over the years as mentor-mentee, he'd never keep secrets from Raven, especially if he believed the information would protect Juni.

Gah.

She couldn't even get angry at the loyalty. It's how every single other member of the Crawford family operated, and that's exactly who Rourke was to all of them. Family.

She already had two annoying older brothers. Adding an additional one had been an easy transition.

Sort of.

Once she managed to get over that massive crush.

"Looks like we'll have to cut our moose hunting trip short." Rourke examined the bodies.

"Why would we do that?" These guys already tried to kill her and failed. "Why should they get to impede the investigation any more than they already have?"

"Because I have to take these men back to the fortress to see if they can be identified, and I'm not leaving you out in the open," Rourke said half in words, half in a growl.

"They look like guild assassins to me," Lincoln said.

She didn't want to know how he knew that, but Cole, her brother-in-law had established the guild and Rourke, their trainer, was an ex-guild assassin. One of them, or both, had probably taken him on a little field trip.

Without her.

"Assholes," she muttered under her breath.

Rourke and Lincoln shared a look, and their mouths split into almost identical grins. They didn't need to read her mind to follow her train of thought.

"Do you recognize any of them?" Lincoln asked Rourke.

The guardian shook his head. "But that means very little. I haven't been a part of the guild for six years."

"High turnover rate?" Juni batted her eyelashes because she couldn't resist the opportunity to annoy her mentor.

Rourke scowled.

"Juni and I can stay and keep looking," Lincoln said.

Juni flashed him a giant smile. He just earned some brownie points.

Lincoln winked.

"So the two of you can make out until another assassin gets close enough to stab one of you?" Rourke shoved his cleaned daggers away. "Not a chance."

"I'm a fierce, independent woman." Juni drew up straight, prepared to launch into a lecture about being an adult capable of making her own decisions when Rourke turned to her.

"They sent five guild-level assassins for you, princess," he said. "Come back to the Shadow Court. Please."

The please got her.

She shut her mouth and nodded, stepping into the portal the second Rourke opened it.

# CHAPTER 12

"What do you call a sleepy male moose?"
(Dramatic pause)
"A bull-dozer."

— JUNI'S DAD

When Juni caught the scent of the mystery moose the next day, hope and fear washed through her body. This was it. Her chance to exonerate her friend.

The smell of fermented apples and Quinn's blood lingered with the moose's scent. Hopefully, enough physical evidence remained on the moose for the police once she delivered the prime suspect. Questions teased her brain as she stomped through the forest. Why hadn't the shifter showered? Why had they stayed in the area? She'd expected faint traces, but when they started out from the orchard, she'd found a new trail that packed a powerful, recent punch. Why had the shifter revisited the crime scene? Surely, they weren't that stupid.

She picked up the pace and found the moose in a clearing about an hour's walk south of the orchard.

"That's a whole fucking moose," Lincoln said.

"Definitely not a shifter," Juni agreed.

"What the fuck is wrong with it?" Rourke asked.

They watched the moose with blood-stained antlers stumble around the moss-covered clearing.

"Is it..." Lincoln tilted his head and leaned forward. "Is it drunk?"

The moose leaned against a tree and rocked back and forth. Tilting its head up to the sky, it bayed like some sort of banshee climaxing.

If the moose wasn't drunk, something was seriously wrong with it.

"How does a moose get drunk?" Rourke rarely appeared confused.

Mauling and stomping on a human wouldn't make the moose act this way, and the only other clear scent she pulled from the air was the apples. The moose clearly enjoyed eating them, even if they had fermented in the heat.

Fermented.

Of course.

"The fermented apples." Juni snapped her fingers.

"And it went back for more?" Lincoln widened his eyes

"So we're dealing with a murderous alcoholic moose?" Rourke looked at the sky as if divine intervention would save him from this moment. "And we have to deliver said drunk moose to the local authorities?"

Rather silly of him to pray toward the sky since Juni was the granddaughter of a god and standing right beside him.

Lincoln clasped Rourke's shoulder. "You've fallen so low."

Rourke grumbled and shrugged away Lincoln's hand. He didn't bother trying to hide the tug on his lips. For all his whining, Rourke enjoyed every second of this.

"I'll get Cole." Rourke disappeared through a portal.

Lincoln leaned in and brushed her cheek with the back of his finger. "It's going to be okay, Juni. You did it. You found the moose. Dani is going to be okay."

She leaned into him, and he wrapped his arms around her. With her face pressed against the hard leather straps of his armour, she inhaled deeply. He smelled like leather and iron all the time—a smell she'd come to associate with him.

Rourke popped back into existence a few feet away, a rope clasped in one hand.

"Where's Cole?" she asked, not moving.

Lincoln's arms tightened around her.

"With your sister. They've gone to the troll kingdom," he answered. "To help them."

"Voluntarily?" She lifted her head from Lincoln's chest.

To put it lightly, her sister had a tumultuous past with the trolls. Not Raven's fault, the trolls had started it. Raven just finished it.

"Apparently," Rourke said.

"Without you?" Lincoln's chest rumbled against hers.

"Obviously."

She bit her lip and swallowed the laughter threatening to bubble out of her mouth.

Rourke must be pissed. He hated the trolls for trying to ambush Raven all those years ago, and not only did her sister run off to help them, she'd left Rourke behind.

Lincoln dropped his arms to release her and stepped away, taking his deliciously familiar scent with him. "So we have to lead a drunk moose through the forest to the police station on our own?"

Rourke grimaced and held up the rope.

They turned in unison toward the moose. Still downwind, the big boy should've detected them by now but from all appearances remained oblivious to their presence. He'd abandoned his scratching post and now stood in the middle of the clearing with his knees locked, swaying side to side. His wide-set eyes fixated on the treeline above him, and a cloud of vapour vented from his nostrils in the morning air. A branch had somehow got stuck in his large antlers along with what looked and smelled like Quinn's flesh and blood. The velvet covering his antlers, normally soft and fuzzy, appeared matted with blood. The fur on his head, dewlap and hump were also caked with blood.

Lots of blood.

Everywhere.

"At least he's been too busy getting drunk on apples to wash off the evidence," Lincoln said.

"Better save that optimism," Juni said. "We're going to need it to get this guy to the police station."

"Why don't we get him to the cabin's orchard instead?" Lincoln asked. "It shouldn't be as hard to lead him back to his booze stash and then we can call the police from the cabin."

She liked that idea a lot more than her own. "I'm so thankful you're not just a pretty face."

Rourke groaned.

Today was looking up.

# CHAPTER 13

"What did the moose say when it got caught?"
(Dramatic pause)
"There's been a moose-take."

— JUNI'S DAD

Today had to be one of the worst days of her life—not because she found it overly traumatizing, but because she hadn't felt so stupid and uncoordinated since high school.

Getting the rope around the inebriated moose had proven a tad more difficult than any of them originally anticipated.

"Just let me stab him." Rourke said. He leaned against a nearby tree with his arms folded across his chest. He'd refused to try to lasso the moose after Juni and Lincoln both failed. He might act like he was above it all, but really, he probably didn't want to end up covered in dirt like them.

He also *accidentally* sent a video to the family group chat of Juni face-planting during her last failed attempt to rope a moose.

Dad was losing it. He bombarded her phone with every moose joke in his arsenal. Her phone pinged again, and she stoically ignored it.

"We could go back to the castle and round up some help," Lincoln suggested.

"And have more witnesses to this?" Juni scoffed. "Absolutely not."

Lincoln brushed off the dirt caked to his leather armour and held out the rope. "Then you're up."

She snatched the rope from his hand and turned to the moose. "No videotaping this time."

"Better move quick," Rourke said. "I think he's sobering up."

She scowled at the guardian and pulled on her magic. Time to try something different.

Her magic looped around the teetering moose while a song slipped from her lips. She didn't know the words and every time she tried to focus on the lyrics, the song fell away. Shaking her head, she let the magic pour from her and tried not to think about it too much. Slowly approaching the moose, she let her magic soak into the animal.

He stayed mostly still, swaying only a little, but

he'd been rocking back and fore before she started. With a deep breath, she lobbed the rope over the moose's neck.

No reaction.

She ducked under his massive head and grabbed the loose end. The smell of fermented apples and dried blood intensified. Looping the end around the rope she held, Juni tied a knot.

Done.

She'd roped the moose, and she hadn't face-planted in the dirt. She turned to the men, holding the end of the rope up triumphantly. Her magic fell away, spilling onto the trampled ground like fairy dust,

Rourke frowned.

Lincoln's eyes widened. "Uh...Juni."

Warm air fanned the back of her neck.

She turned slowly.

The moose had come out of his trance and now stood so close she had an excellent view of his gigantic nostrils.

"Uh-oh."

The moose bolted.

Juni had half a second to process that she still held the other end of the rope before she was yanked from her spot. She flew through the air, holding onto rope for her life.

She refused to let go.

This stupid moose meant her friend's freedom.

She tried to sing again. Her magic slipped away.

Again, she tried, but her body slammed into the side of the moose, knocking the air from her lungs.

"Juni!" The men called out somewhere behind her. She had no idea if they followed or collapsed in fits of laughter.

She smashed against the ground, the impact jarring her teeth. The moose made a sharp turn, sending her flying into the trees. She winced as pain shot up her leg. The rope burned her palms. With clenched teeth and determination, she held on and tried not to get trampled.

The moose's hooves thundered into the ground.

Juni's head pounded. Her body ached. Her hands cramped and threatened to let go, the sweat making her grip slick.

She took short breaths to get air back in her lungs and control her breathing. With her magic unleashed, she sang again, using the power to calm the moose. He slowed. His gallop turned into a trot, then a walk, and finally, he came to a stop.

Her heart beat so loudly it consumed all her senses. How long had he run? It felt like hours, but it couldn't have been that long.

She kept her magic wound around the panting animal—she wouldn't make that mistake twice—and clambered to her feet.

Rourke and Lincoln stepped from a portal a few feet away. The lazy bastards didn't look winded at all.

Had they even tried to keep up? Or did they plan all along to portal to the beacon in her choker?

She glared at them.

Lincoln shrugged.

Rourke ignored her and scanned the area. "Well, that's one way to lead the moose back to the orchard."

She followed his gaze, and her mouth dropped open.

Sure enough, they stood a few feet away from the edge of the same orchard where Quinn lost his life.

She should've noticed the increased intensity of fermented apples in the air, but in her defence, she'd been trying not to die or break something.

"I'm fine, by the way," she said.

"Of course, you are," Rourke said. "You're a fierce, independent woman."

The moose huffed and brought his head down to snuffle a rotting apple.

She pulled on the rope. "Don't even think about it."

# CHAPTER 14

"Why shouldn't you kiss someone on January 1$^{st}$?"
(Dramatic pause)
"Because it's the first date."

— JUNI'S DAD

J uni stepped from the steamy bathroom and scrunched her hair in the towel. She'd spent longer than usual in the shower, because scraping the grime, sap, fur, and pine needles from her bruised body had been infuriating and time consuming. Now, her skin glowed a nice angry red that almost matched her hair. At least she was clean.

Explaining to the Okanagan police why she'd roped a drunken moose to their crime scene had taken most of the night and a good chunk of the next day. The RCMP still hadn't officially dropped the charges against Dani, but she'd done what she could do. At least for now. If they still went ahead with their anti-shifter nonsense, she'd go with Rourke's plan and break Dani out of jail once she inevitably got thrown in there.

Thoughts of her friend fled from her mind when she realized she wasn't alone.

Lincoln stood in the middle of the bedroom, his dark hair still damp from his own shower. He must've let himself in after he finished.

She scanned the room. "Where's the babysitter?"

Kind of unfair to call Rourke that, he was a lot more than a nursemaid, but lately it felt like he didn't trust her on her own with only Lincoln to protect her, despite the arrangement being the status quo for years.

"Even legends need a break, apparently."

"The moose rustling really did him in. How long do you think we have?"

"Maybe an hour."

"I can't believe he's left us alone." She tossed the towel in a basket by the door. This wasn't her usual room. This one was nestled deep within the Corvid Court behind even more walls of enchantment and layers of protection.

And it had no balcony.

Rourke looked entirely too pleased when he led her to this place, and it definitely felt more like a vault than a bedroom. If she wasn't careful, he'd surround her with bubble wrap, too.

Lincoln ran his hand through his hair. He'd decided on reg clothing—a simple T-shirt and faded jeans that did nothing to hide his powerful body.

She licked her lips.

Lincoln caught the movement, and his gaze snagged on her mouth. "I can go, if you want. You haven't really been left alone since..."

"Since Bane."

"Yeah." He jammed his hands in his pockets and shifted his weight from foot to foot. "Did you want to rest? Be alone?"

"Not at all."

He hesitated. "I know we've gone over a lot of what happened after you became Bane's guardian, but you haven't said very much about the cabin. Bane didn't hurt you, did he?" His expression softened, but he couldn't hide how his shoulders tensed.

"He didn't do a thing. I didn't talk about the cabin because I wasn't there for very long and nothing happened. I sat around and read disturbing plaques."

Bane had given her a tour of the place at the start, too. She'd even spied a framed picture by his bedside of some unknown woman—probably a lover from another lifetime he liked to think of occasionally to remember the time when he had a heart.

Juni closed the distance between her and Lincoln and placed her hands flat on his chest. He was so strong. *He was her strength, and she was his weakness.*

"Juni?"

"Hmm?"

He finally pulled his hands free from his pockets and settled them on her hips. "Why were the plaques disturbing? Did they have scenes of massacres or sadistic quotes?"

She chuckled and leaned in to press her forehead on his chest.

He automatically dropped his chin to rest on the top of her head and slipped his hands over her butt to pull her in for a hug.

"The plaques themselves aren't disturbing," she mumbled into his warmth. His familiar scent curled around her. "They are more like things a forty-year-old woman would get to stage a room for social media pictures."

Lincoln chuckled, his hands tightening on her butt. He dropped his head to nuzzle her neck and drop kisses on the sensitive skin. "Not something you'd expect from the Lord of War."

"Exactly." She tilted her head to the side and closed her eyes, enjoying the feel of Lincoln's mouth on her skin. "Did you want to keep talking about Bane, or...?"

"Absolutely not." His mouth found hers and with a flick of his tongue, he made her forget what they just talked about.

She melted into him, kissing him back, tasting his lips. She wanted his hands and mouth all over her. She wanted to feel him, claim him, and make him truly hers. She tugged at his shirt, and he broke their kiss long enough to pull off the clothing. His muscles rippled with the movement and then she was back in his arms.

Her magic spilled out. She mumbled a song against Lincoln's lips.

He smiled and moved his mouth to her jaw and neck. "I love it when you sing."

She had no idea what the words meant or what song slipped from her lips, but it didn't affect Lincoln the same way it had the fae who'd attacked her. It spiraled around him, caressing his skin.

She tugged his belt free and pulled his jeans down. The belt hit the floor first, with a loud thud. His pants fell next, the cloth whispering to the cold stone floor before settling.

She froze. "You're not wearing any underwear."

He was gloriously naked, and she wanted to push away from him so she could have an unobstructed view.

His mouth twitched on her skin. "I feel like you're woefully overdressed right now."

He stepped back, gaze wild, her magic wrapped around him.

She reached out to run her hands along his shoulders. The cut from the assassin's blade had completely healed.

She jerked back.

A white line marked the place where the dagger had sliced through his skin, but otherwise, the wound had healed.

Like, *completely* healed

"The cut. It's healed."

He looked down at his shoulder and ran his fingers along the scar "That takes sexual healing up a notch."

She gulped.

He turned his attention back to hers, his gaze darkening. "You're some sort of empathic mage, or a siren. I wonder what else your magic does."

"When we have sex," she finished his thought in her mind.

Her body almost split in two from warring emotions—excitement and fear.

She stepped backward,

"Juni?" Lincoln frowned.

She took another step. Her lungs felt tight. She couldn't breathe.

Concern pierced Lincoln's expression. "What's wrong?"

"I'm sorry," she mumbled. What was happening? Why was it suddenly so hard to breathe?

"What did I do?"

Nothing. He did nothing wrong.

She threw down the lodestone and stepped into the waiting swirls of gray.

"Juni!" Lincoln could've easily followed her through the portal, but he held back, either too dumbfounded to move or he respected her need for space.

The moment she stepped from the portal and onto her parents' front lawn, she knew she'd made a mistake.

# CHAPTER 15

"Your sister keeps judging people on their sound
systems."
(Dramatic pause)
"I told her to stop being so stereotypical."

— JUNI'S DAD

"Stupid." Juni cursed. "Stupid, stupid, stupid."

She stomped up the front stairs. She was *that* girl. The one who fled from situations instead of facing them. She'd never been that girl before. Not for a day in her life. Until now. Until she faced Lincoln with all these intense and new feelings.

She slammed shut the front door behind her. Familiar and unfamiliar scents from the kitchen travelled down the hallway.

Juni growled. Of course, she wasn't alone. Of course, there'd be someone home to witness her moment of sheer weakness and stupidity.

She treaded heavily down the hallway and froze. She'd expected her sister and two strangers from their scents, but not a mother and son.

The boy sitting at the table didn't look up from his tablet at her entrance, but his mom turned to her with a haunted expression.

Huh.

Juni had never met this woman, but something familiar about her face tugged at her mind.

"Everything okay?" Raven asked. She wore jeans and a T-shirt and looked nothing like what most regs would expect the Queen of Corvids to look like.

"Nothing is okay," she said. Ugh. She didn't feel like dishing everything that just happened. Rourke and Cole must've kept the information about the assassins from Raven, or maybe there hadn't been time or opportunity to tell her. If Raven knew about the attacks, she'd ask Juni why she wasn't at the castle under protection.

Without another word, Juni headed for her basement bedroom.

Stomping down the stairs did nothing to alleviate the self-loathing. Juni pushed one of the armchairs over and launched into an advanced fae dagger kata.

As she moved through the predetermined combination of turns, blocks and strikes, she regained control of her breathing and tried to calm her mind.

Lincoln wanted to have sex with her. That wasn't the shocking or upsetting part.

She never wanted someone the way she wanted that man. Instead of stepping up, though, she ran away from her fears. Like a chump. Like a scared child. She was past letting fear rule her life.

Raven had made her way to the bottom of the stairs outside the room, her unique scent slipping under the bedroom door and announcing her presence long before she knocked.

"It's me," Raven said.

Of course, it was. Maybe if Juni kept focused on her kata, her older sister would go away.

The door creaked open, and Raven popped her head in. "I expected to find you crying into a pillow." She swung the door open fully to lean on the door jam.

"Do you know me at all? What do you want?" Juni finished the kata with a bow and flinched. Her words and tone were harsher than Raven deserved.

"I want to know what's up with you and whether I can do anything to help."

"What's up with me?" So much. Too much. And she didn't want to talk about any of it. "What's up with you?" Juni winced again. Two for two. She acted like a total cow. Apparently, she didn't work well with self-inflicted humiliation.

Her sister pinned her with a look. "Does this have anything to do with Lincoln?"

Juni's face heated. Oh, for fuck's sake. Why was this her life? Why did everyone have to know her business?

Her sister's expression softened.

Juni paused long enough to take a deep breath. Maybe the world wouldn't end if she asked for a little bit of help. Out of all her siblings, Raven was by far the snarkiest, but she was also the most compassionate and empathetic.

"I don't know what to do about it," she said.

"About Lincoln?"

"No. It." She waved her daggers in the air. Sex. Odin's shriveled ball sack, please let her sister figure this one out without her having to elaborate.

"You're not making any sense," Raven said. "Why don't you put the knives down so we can talk about it without me risking a stab wound?"

Juni certainly felt like stabbing something at the moment. She looked around the room for answers. Raven had converted their parents' basement into a giant suite years ago and after she moved out to shack up with Cole, Juni had claimed the space. She'd decorated with soft white Christmas lights and had her own bedding but had otherwise kept things pretty much the same.

Raven took a seat in one of the leather armchairs and waited.

Dang it. There'd be no shooing her away now.

Juni slapped her weapons on the top of the nearby dresser and sat in the other chair with enough force to make it creak.

Raven waited expectantly.

May as well get on with this. "I've never done it."

Raven might've tried to keep her expression neutral, but confusion flashed across her face for a brief second. She took a moment, as if selecting her words carefully. "Do you want to do it?"

Odin's balls, this was mortifying. "Yes."

"With Lincoln?"

She nodded. *Just kill me now.*

"So what's the problem?"

What was the problem? Raven wanted only one? Juni ran through the gamut of emotions trying to pinpoint a singular source. "What if I suck at it?"

Raven bit her lip. "I'm pretty sure Lincoln would enjoy that."

Yup. Dead. Someone needed to pull the plug. Juni leapt up from the chair and started pacing. Her sister might think this funny, but Juni had to talk to someone. "I'm serious, Rayray. What if...What if I'm bad at it? I've never met anyone I've wanted to go there with before, and now I feel like I'm going into battle unprepared." *What if I'm bad at it? What if I don't like it? What if I lose Lincoln over it?*

There.

She said it.

Well, most of it.

The truth was out.

Raven cocked her head at her like one of her birds. "Did you run off on Lincoln?"

Juni winced and nodded.

"The first thing you need to do is talk to him. Communicate."

Juni's stomach sunk. Even the less logical part of Juni's brain registered the importance of communication, and she'd anticipated Raven dishing out something along these lines. The words weren't surprising but knowing something was the right thing to do and actually doing it were two entirely different things.

"I know," Raven said, voice soft. "It's not my specialty either. But Lincoln should know, and I think discussing your feelings with him might put you at ease, and it will also help him understand why you ran off."

Or...she could just move away to another city and avoid him for the rest of her life. He probably hated her now. "What if he doesn't want me?"

"He does."

"But what if?" What if he changed his mind? What if he saw her naked and didn't want her anymore? What if she caused more drama than what she was worth?

"Then he's a moron and not worth your time," Raven said, very matter-of-factly.

Juni stopped pacing and nodded to herself. She wasn't usually prone to so much self-consciousness. She normally had more confidence, more self-esteem. Chartering this unknown territory really had her off her game.

"Sex isn't like some kata, Juni. There are no pre-set movements or requirements. Talk to Lincoln and have fun," Raven said.

"Have fun?"

"Yes. Have fun. It's meant to be enjoyable. Finding out what you like and what your partner likes is half the thrill. Tormenting them with the knowledge is the other half."

Juni's face screwed up. "Odin's shrivelled nuggets, you're actually making sense."

"I do that sometimes."

*Not often.* Juni bit back the snarky response, and instead, asked, "Can we forget this conversation ever happened?"

"Not a chance."

Dang it.

Juni flopped back into the armchair. Her phone vibrated in her pocket. She pulled it free and saw Lincoln's name flash across the screen.

Oh no.

Not yet.

She had to pull up her lady socks first and now was not the time.

Raven rose from the chair, her scent toying with

Juni's senses. Did her sister know why her scent had changed, yet? Should Juni tell her?

Her older sister paused at the door and turned back to her. "Remember, just talk to him. Preferably in person."

Juni slid the phone onto the surface of the coffee table between them, her mind already scrambling through possible ways to reach out to Lincoln. Conversation starters. A script where she spun her moment of panic and insecurity in some positive way.

Raven was right, she needed to speak with Lincoln in person. And privately. Certainly not in front of her sister.

"Who are the strangers upstairs?" Juni asked, needing to change the subject.

"Kayden Smith and his mother, Felicia Johnson," Raven answered without hesitation.

Kayden Smith?

Her mind placed the name in a millisecond. When Bane absconded her to the Realm of War and before the family became aware of her situation, Mike, her brother and partner in crime-solving, had taken a missing person's case—Kayden Smith. The father hired Crawford Investigations to locate his missing son. The news outlets had flashed Kayden's face everywhere since he went missing a few weeks ago. Maybe that's why his mom looked so familiar.

And apparently, in between trying to find a way to

break her bond with Bane and visiting the troll domain, Raven had also been helping Mike with the case.

"You closed the case?" Juni asked. Finally. A win. She needed that.

"Yes. Sort of."

Something still nagged at Juni's brain. Her memory. The mom. Had Mike shown her a picture of Kayden's mother? No. He couldn't have. He'd barely had time to mention the case before she left to help Dani. Had the media shown her picture?

Picture.

Picture...

Wait a hot second.

"Why do you look like you've sucked on a lemon?" Raven asked.

"The mom looks familiar. I was trying to place her face. Bane has a picture in his cabin of a similar looking woman."

"How similar?" Raven straightened, her gaze narrowing on Juni with hyper focus. Not even something shiny could distract her sister when she focused like this. When Raven gave her this look, Juni swore she felt the weight of her entire conspiracy and the power of the Shadow Realm focused on her.

"Same woman, just different clothes or with a different expression similar?" Raven continued. "Or sister similar? Distant relation?"

"I don't know. I've been blocking memories of that creepy place."

"Did you see the plaques?"

"Of course, I saw those fucking plaques." She paused, mentally flicking through the details of the cabin. "Do you think he hung them himself or got some poor servant from the Realm of War to do it?"

"I don't know. I got through my time there by imagining a big, badass dark fae warrior whose only dream growing up was to serve the mighty lord, but after he worked hard to rise through the ranks, he discovered he landed an interior decorating gig to the most neurotic sociopath in existence."

Juni laughed. If only she had the same overactive imagination as her sister. Her time at the cabin would've gone faster. "Poor dark fae underling."

Her phone vibrated on the table. She didn't need to pick it up to know who was calling.

"I'll leave you to it." Raven turned away.

Juni half-heartedly flipped up her middle finger at her sister's back, not because she actually meant it, but because Raven didn't bother to hide her chuckle. At this point, Juni's immature behaviour was practically expected.

Magic spread through the room tingling Juni's senses. Familiar unwelcomed magic. Something tugged on her bond with Bane. She straightened and watched a portal open in the middle of her basement bedroom.

"Time to go, my little vixen." Bane stepped from the red haze.

Seriously? This guy had the worse timing. She glanced down at her phone. "Right now?"

"I'm heading to court. You must attend me." He held out his hand expectantly.

He obviously had the roles of servant and guardian confused.

"What in the Underworld, Bane." Raven folded her arms over her chest. "You survived how long without a caomhnóir? Surely, you're not so weak as to need her now."

Oh no. Raven could not step in for her. Not in her condition. Juni would do anything to prevent a fight from breaking out. Anything to keep her sister safe.

Juni plucked her daggers off the nearby dresser and sheathed them.

"Trying to shame me into leaving your sister here?" He shook his finger at Raven. "Tsk. Tsk. Raven dearest. You wound me. And here I thought we were basically family."

"Family doesn't torment one another." Raven said.

Juni winced.

"Have you seen your family interact?" Bane widened his eyes.

"Not seriously torment each other," Raven amended, but her point had been lost. "You don't need Juni."

"You're right," Bane said. "But I want her, and she's mine now. You're in no position to barter."

Raven wasn't in a position to barter, but she was in

a position to fight, shifting her weight and unfolding her arms. Raven wouldn't kill Bane because that would kill Juni, but the ice in her sister's eyes said Raven was prepared to maim and mutilate.

"It's okay, Rayray," Juni said. "I'll go."

Raven snarled.

"He can't force me to stay with him at all times. I'll be back." Despite every warning system she possessed screaming at her to run away and find Lincoln, she stepped toward the Lord of War and slapped her hand in his.

The smug bastard had the nerve to wink at Raven before pulling Juni through the portal with him to the Underworld.

# CHAPTER 16

"Thor, Loki and Odin walked into a bar."
(Dramatic pause)
"I ducked."

— JUNI'S DAD

J uni stepped from the angry red haze and shook the feeling of rage from her skin. Unlike the cold detachment of Cole's shadow portals or the oddly comforting ones of Raven's that mixed shadows and chaotic corvid essence, Bane's portals would slowly drive her to madness with the pain and rage burning her skin.

Maybe that's why Bane was the way he was. Maybe his method of transportation left him chronically cranky.

Juni stared at the large fortress in front of her. "Is this..."

"Odin's Hall. Yes. Your sister's grandfather is expecting us." Bane strolled past her, shoulders loose, gait easy. "Hurry up."

The red moons of the Underworld bathed her in warm light and illuminated the stone path that led to the entrance of the fortress. Two oversized wolves sat at the top of the stairs under an archway. Sounds of shattering plates, clinking glass, loud shouts and boisterous laughter spilled from the open doors to Odin's Hall.

She turned to Bane. "The big bad Lord of War couldn't plunk us in the center of the hall for a grand entrance?"

Bane scoffed. "Of course not. The main hall is shielded, and I don't plan to start a war with Odin."

"Isn't that your thing?"

He narrowed his eyes at her. "My *thing* is to wage wars and win. Needlessly inciting Odin's anger isn't a smart move."

"Your thing sounds awfully close to caution or cowardice." She bit her lip and had to look away from the fury that sparked in Bane's gaze.

"My thing is impressive," he growled. "Now get a move on. The only thing dumber than portalling into Odin's Hall is making him wait."

He walked beside her as they made their way up the stairs, past the wolves and into the fortress.

Battered shields lined the walls and swords hung overhead as rafters. The air smelled of metal, wood, sweat and earth, and drifted to her nose in swaths of heat along with the unique scent signatures of the warriors in the room. Fire pits crackled down the centre of the hall, their light reflected by the gold roof to illuminate the room even more.

Bane took the aisle that ran along the right of the fire pits and ignored the battle-worn warriors who sat at tables covered with toppling piles of food. Most of them continued to eat, laugh and shout at one another, but they all watched Bane and her progress through the hall.

Bane and Juni stopped at the end of the aisle when they reached the bottom steps of a dais. Her vision wavered. Had she held her breath this entire time? The two wolves, presumably from outside, brushed past them and bounded up the steps to flop down at the feet of the man sitting on a large throne made of skulls. A pair of ravens perched on the man's broad shoulders and snapped their heads in her direction, scanning her with their beady eyes.

She tugged on Bane's sleeve and leaned in. "What are we doing here?"

"Yes, Bane," Odin spoke over the din in the hall. "What are you doing here?"

Odin had wrapped his long, blood-red cloak around himself, hiding whatever body armour he wore. Raven had always described Odin as Santa Claus's wayward brother who fell off the sleigh, pumped a shit-load of iron straight into his veins, and fought for the wrong side in a turf war. And she wasn't wrong.

Nailed it.

A long scar ran from the middle of Odin's fore-head, over his milky white eye, to mid-cheek and added to his sinister expression. His lip curled up over his teeth as he waited for Bane to answer.

"You invited me." Bane waved a black business card in his hand. She'd seen one like it years ago, when Raven found one in Bear's mail.

The Allfather leaned forward in his seat.

The two ravens perched on the back of his throne continued to blink at her. Huginn and Muninn, thought and memory, Odin's spies, and most impor-tantly, when combined to form one massive warrior, Raven and Bear's biological father—Huginn Muninn.

Mom had a rebellious past.

"I'm aware I granted you an audience," Odin said. "Why have you shown up with my grandchildren's half-sister?"

The room grew silent. No one had paid them much attention before. Bantering between dark fae gods and lords must be fairly commonplace, but a fox shifter, half-sibling of the Queen of Corvids showing up in Odin's Hall...not so much.

Every single set of eyes in the hall settled on her. Not all the gazes of the dark fae in Odin's Hall were hostile, but they weren't all friendly either. Why couldn't she just disappear? The urge to shift and hide thrummed in her veins while her magic pulsed, aching to be let out and sing these fools a song.

That couldn't happen. If Bane knew of her burgeoning powers to render opponents useless, he'd never let her go.

"Surely, you wouldn't deny me the presence of my caomhnóir," Bane said.

Somehow the silence became more deafening, smothering the room like the air had been sucked out.

"What are you doing?" she hissed.

Bane shrugged as if completely oblivious to the change in the room. He leaned in to whisper, "My sweet vixen. Sometimes things have nothing to do with you."

She narrowed her eyes at him.

"I'm speeding things up," he said.

Odin's lip peeled back in a snarl. "Your caomhnóir?"

"Trained by one of the best weapon-warpers in the realm." He patted her shoulder, and she stamped down the urge to bite his hand. "Frankly, I think I got one *hell* of a deal."

She hated him.

She absolutely, one hundred percent loathed the man she stood beside. Not only did he talk about her as if she didn't stand right here, not only did he speak about her as if she were some sort of used good, like a car, but revealing their connection just enlarged the target on her back. She hadn't told him about the attacks, yet, but he had spies everywhere. He knew. He had to.

And he didn't give a fuck.

Juni didn't have illusions about her role in this courtroom, but it was one thing to know she was just a game piece on Bane's board game, and another to be made to feel like a pawn.

Ugh.

"Your guardian looks about ready to kill you herself." Odin still hadn't glanced her way and for that she was grateful. She could only handle so much judgement in one day.

"She requires a little training," Bane said.

Odin flashed his teeth, the movement not a smile so much as a promise of malice. "I can help with that."

Oh no.

"Huginn." He looked over one shoulder. "Muninn." He looked over his other shoulder. "I have things to discuss with Bane in private. Please see to Juniper's training."

The two birds launched from the throne. With a loud crack, they collided to form one of the largest fae warriors Juni had ever seen.

Wearing dark matte armour similar to Cole's, Huginn Muninn walked down the remaining stairs, his cape of black feathers trailing behind him. He stopped a few feet in front of her. She hadn't interacted much with Raven and Bear's biological father. Her dad would always be their dad. That was never a question, but in his own way, Huginn Muninn still looked out for their family, especially Raven and Bear.

Huginn Muninn glared down at Bane before holding his arm out to her. "If you would follow me."

"Careful with the goods there," Bane said in warning, acting particularly obnoxious, even for him. What was he getting at? Bane was an ass, but he was a calculating ass. He'd upped his douche bag game the second they stepped from the portal. And he must have a reason for it.

She just needed to figure out that reason.

Juni wrapped her arm around Huginn Muninn's and let him lead her away, pausing only to glare at Bane.

He winked.

Ugh.

Bane said earlier he was trying to speed things up. What in the Underworld did that mean? And why did that do the opposite of reassuring her?

# CHAPTER 17

"Do you know why I like jokes about tea?"
(Dramatic pause)
"They'll have you laughing for oolong time."

— JUNI'S DAD

Juni took in the private room with a wide stone balcony overlooking the ocean below. Huginn Muninn had led her to this place and then called for tea.

Tea.

While they waited, she roamed around the room, and her sister's biological father sat at a small table near the doors to the balcony. Fresh air with hints of ocean spray and a sweet spice flowed over her.

"No inquisition?" she asked over her shoulder.

Before he could answer her, a man in full armour walked into the room with a tray carrying a white tea pot and two china cups.

Huginn Muninn waved at the table, and the scowl on the man's face deepened. The nameless soldier placed the tray down in front of Huginn Muninn, the teacups clattering.

"That is all," Huginn Muninn said.

The man stalked away and shut the door behind him. He hadn't spoken a word and had avoided eye contact the entire time.

"What did he do to earn tea duty?" Juni asked. The dark fae was obviously being punished for something.

Huginn Muninn smiled and waved at the empty chair across from him. "He made disparaging remarks about your sister. I make a point of ordering tea every time I'm in this form."

Juni pulled out the other chair and sat down. "I'm surprised he's alive."

"Odin wouldn't let me kill him."

"Boo."

Huginn Muninn smiled again with the patience of an ancient old fae in a young man's body and poured her a cup of black tea before pouring his own.

"I know we have not conversed a lot over the years, but you are my daughter's beloved sister, and I have watched you grow up from a baby. My daughter held you and played with you and has loved you since you arrived in this world kicking and screaming." He conveniently left out the part where he watched over them partly because he was still in love with Mom, but that was fine with Juni. She'd already reached her quota for awkward conversations today.

She reached forward and poured milk into her tea before stirring in a small spoonful of sugar.

"You have grown into a capable, sensible young woman," he said. "What in the Mortal Realm possessed you to bond your life to..."

The air stirred. An incoming portal formed. Entering directly into Odin's domain shouldn't be possible. At least that's what she grasped from what little Bane told her. So who formed a portal now? Only those with permission or those with special tracker lodestones like the one connected to her choker could breach the Allfather's sanctum.

She fumbled to place her teacup down. Creamy brown liquid sloshed over the side as Lincoln stepped from the portal.

He had a fraction of a second to take in the room and widen his eyes before Huginn Muninn was on him, pinning him to the wall with a dagger at his throat.

"No!" Juni cried.

Huginn Muninn snarled over his shoulder, his eyes bleeding out to full black.

"He's with me. He works for Raven."

Huginn Muninn hesitated before stepping back, keeping the sharp edge of the blade on Lincoln.

Lincoln held still, his gaze darting between her and Huginn Muninn.

"Now that you mention it, he does look familiar." Huginn Muninn leaned in and sniffed. "Are you that scrap of a boy Raven should've killed all those years ago?"

Lincoln swallowed. Huginn Muninn's blade scraped his skin as his Adam's apple bobbed up and down. "Yeah, that's me."

"Why are you here?"

Lincoln shifted his gaze to meet hers. A swell of emotion spread across his face.

"Oh." Huginn Muninn stepped farther back, and he removed his dagger. "I see."

Did he? From the sad look he quickly hid with a stony mask, he just might.

"Do you want to speak with him?" Huginn Muninn jerked his chin at Lincoln just in case there was any doubt to whom he referred. "Or should I stab him?"

She wanted to speak to Lincoln alone and at home, relaxed and in the comfort of her own room, but sometimes life had other ideas.

"I'd like to speak with him," she said. "No stabbing required."

"If you change your mind, let me know." Huginn Muninn spun and left the room, his tea untouched and forgotten.

He probably didn't even like tea.

"Raven's biological father is scary as fuck." A little droplet of blood trickled down his neck. Coming from a reg who regularly trained with fae assassins that said a lot.

She tilted her head and considered the door the man had left through. "I find him kind of endearing..."

"Is that where we are? Odin's hall?" Lincoln looked around the room.

She nodded.

"Why would Bane bring you here?"

"I'm not sure. Apparently, he woke up this morning and decided to up his game for being the Underworld's biggest asshole. Guess he felt he needed to accessorize with his one and only guardian."

Silence answered her, an uncomfortable weight in the air.

Lincoln hesitated, seemingly unsure of how to proceed. He inhaled a deep breath, took three steps to close the distance between them and gathered her hands in his. "I don't know what I did, but I want you to tell me so I can apologize and do better."

Oh, okay. They were going to get right into it.

"It's me who should apologize. I shouldn't have run off like that."

He frowned, and the silence stretched over them when she didn't elaborate.

She didn't know how to.

"Why did you run?" Lincoln prompted.

"I panicked. I would've come right back, but then I

was super embarrassed that I panicked. I was working through how to get back to you without looking like too much of an idiot when Bane hauled me off."

Lincoln squeezed her hands. "Why did you panic? That's not like you. You're the strongest person I know."

She could lie. She could make up some lame excuse or try run away again. But her stupid sister and her stupid advice kept repeating like a broken record in her brain.

"I am a little overwhelmed with how intense my feelings are for you," she admitted.

A pause and then Lincoln smiled. "Those feelings are mutual."

She bit her lip and looked away. "No. You don't understand. I've never felt like this, nor have I ever felt the need to go further with someone."

"Juni." Lincoln wrapped her in his arms, surrounding her with his deliciously familiar scent. His chest rumbled.

She stiffened in his arms. "Are you laughing at me?"

"No. Definitely not." His shoulders shook.

"I'm trying to tell you I'm a virgin and scared, and you're laughing."

He chuckled and dropped his head, so his forehead rested on hers. "Juni. I have been a prisoner in your sister's dungeon since I was fifteen."

"She freed you ages ago."

"After which I devoted my life to guarding you. Exactly how much experience do you think I have, and where do you think I got it?"

She pulled back and met his dancing gaze. "Wait...what?"

He couldn't possibly be saying what she thought he was saying.

"But...your tongue," she said. "The way you kiss me..."

His mouth split into a panty-melting grin.

Before he could say anything more, the door to the room slammed open, and Bane barged in. "Time to go—"

The Lord of War stopped in his tracks and glared at Lincoln. "I suppose you're the one to thank for all the warm fuzzy vibes pulling on our bond."

Lincoln scowled. "You could've shut down the link."

"And miss all this?" Bane smirked. "Time to go, little vixen. Say goodbye to your plaything."

"No." Lincoln straightened.

"No?" Bane's head snapped back as if Lincoln had physically struck him. "No?"

"I'm coming with you," he said.

Bane blinked. "I don't recall inviting you."

"Your guardian did."

Well, technically she hadn't, but she nodded when Bane glanced over at her.

"He'll just follow if you try to leave without him," she added, smiling as widely as possible.

Bane narrowed his eyes.

Anyone else would be scared of Bane, would fear he'd simply kill Lincoln to remove the inconvenience, but Bane didn't kill so easily. He manipulated. He calculated. Simply murdering a reg for insolence wasn't his jam—the act too easy and lacking subtly.

Now, if Lincoln annoyed Bane enough, he might orchestrate his demise through intricate plotting.

Bane was the Lord of War, not Lord of Murder. He needed to play with his victims before annihilating them. Like a giant narcissistic cat.

Bane's eyebrows threatened to burrow into his face.

*That's right, I have your number.*

"Fine," Bane spat and opened a portal to the Realm of War.

# CHAPTER 18

"What shape is a kiss?"
(Dramatic pause)
"A-lip-tickle"

— JUNI'S DAD

Juni sat with Lincoln on the couch across from Bane, the fireplace crackling to her right. Even in summer, the fireplace raged on, perpetually burning a seemingly endless supply of wood. Smelled like magic. The fae probably considered this the Underworld equivalent to a thermostat.

She replayed Bane's response when she'd asked why he'd brought her to Odin's hall.

*"My sweet vixen. Sometimes things have nothing to do with you,"* he'd said. *"I'm speeding things up."*

"What did you mean by speeding things up?" she asked with no preamble.

Lincoln jerked upright beside her.

Bane looked up from the amber fluid in his glass. "There's more at play here, little vixen, than our bond."

"You're involved, so yeah. That's kind of a given," she said.

Lincoln shifted on the cushion beside her and frowned as if to ask why she bothered to question the dark fae lord.

"Your sister needed a little incentive." He shrugged.

"So you've outed me to Odin's Court to incur more enemies and make my sister more stressed out about my situation? I can assure you she's already hit the max on that. She's working as fast as she can on a solution."

He smirked. "It's not really the speed of her actions I'm concerned about. It's the speed at which she'll come to the right decision when she's faced with a choice. I'm giving her the motivation to descend from that moral high ground she insists on sitting upon."

"What in the Underworld does that even mean?"

He smiled, lazy and smug, and her fingers itched to stab him again.

"Were you behind the other two attacks as well?" she asked. "All part of your *motivation*?"

Bane's hand froze halfway to bringing the glass to his mouth. He straightened in his seat. "What?"

The temperature in the room dropped.

"Well, it backfired," she said. "I haven't told Raven about the attacks yet because, unlike you, I don't think she needs more stress in her life. Rourke hasn't said anything as far as I'm aware, either. Raven has enough on her plate." More than she even knew.

"What attacks?" Bane had grown eerily quiet, his gaze hyper fixated on her face.

She refused to squirm in her seat.

"What attacks?" His voice rumbled.

"An assassin breached the Corvid Court and a team of five guild-level fae ambushed us in the Mortal Realm," Lincoln said. Though he'd taken his boots off and leaned back in the sofa, he wasn't relaxed. At all. Tension kept his posture stiff.

"Did they hurt you?" Fury flashed in Bane's gaze.

"Juni wasn't hurt," Lincoln answered for her again, which was probably a good thing because the rage shaking along her bond to Bane rendered her speechless.

Bane squeezed the tumbler so hard it shattered in his hand. Glass sprayed out and amber splashed on the floor near his feet. Blood trickled from his hand, but he kept his gaze locked on her. His pupils bled out, making his eyes all black.

"Where are they?" he spoke so quietly, she almost didn't realize he'd spoken, even with her fox hearing.

"Dead," Lincoln said.

"Good." He shook the blood from his hand and

stood, looming over Juni. "No one harms what is *mine*."

"I'm not yours." Juni lifted her chin. Oh look, she found her voice.

"Your life bound to mine suggests otherwise," he said. "I'm going out. If you know what's best for you, you'll stay here. No one can infiltrate this cabin except me and your family. Don't wait up."

He stomped out of the room and dark fae magic briefly flooded the cabin as he formed a portal to leave.

"That was...intense," Lincoln said.

Understatement of the year.

Juni didn't breathe until the portal snapped shut in the other room, and she was completely alone with Lincoln.

"I thought he'd never leave." Lincoln leaned over and tucked a lock of curly red hair behind her ear. "We haven't finished our conversation from earlier."

What more did he need to say or hear?

"Juni." His gaze danced, the laughter welling up inside him clearly evident. "I think there's a lot more to talk about."

Oops. She must've said that last part out loud.

"I just..." Her brain fumbled for words.

"Get uncomfortable talking about your feelings?"

She nodded.

"I'm surprised you've said this much," he admitted.

"Raven said I should talk to you in person."

His eyebrows rose. "I'm *very* surprised you talked to her about this."

"Are you mad?"

"Not at all. It's just that you're intensely private."

"She got me at a moment of weakness," she admitted.

He swept her hair from her shoulder and leaned in to kiss her neck. "And what did you talk about, exactly?"

Did he seriously want a play by play?

"Yes. Talk to me. Tell me what you told her."

She sighed. She'd said that out loud, too. "She asked me what was wrong. I told her I was scared."

"Of me?"

"No."

"Of rejection? Because I can eliminate that fear very quickly."

"I thought you wanted me to talk?"

"Of course." He kissed her neck again and slid his calloused hand over her thigh.

"I'm scared I'll suck at it."

Lincoln's hand stilled. "What did Raven say?"

"That you'd probably like that."

Lincoln dropped his forehead on her shoulder, his whole body shaking.

"Don't laugh."

The shaking intensified until he straightened. "Well, she's not wrong."

Juni looked up and their gazes locked. His eyes, like deep pools of need and want, transfixed her.

"I'd like that very much," he said.

"Is that so?"

He licked his lips and leaned in again. "There are a lot of things I'd like."

She leaned back, enjoying seeing him like this, unguarded.

"What else did your sister say?" His voice had dropped to a low growl.

"I don't know. I was too embarrassed to pay attention to all of it. Something about katas and training. Blah, blah, blah. I'd rather not go over the conversation word for word. But she told me to have fun."

"Have fun?"

"Yeah. And that finding out what you like is half the fun, and the other half is tormenting you with the knowledge."

Lincoln groaned and flopped back in the couch. "Woman, you already torment me."

"Do I?"

"All the time." His expression grew serious. "I think about you all the time. When I'm awake, when I'm asleep, when I'm in those quiet moments in-between...It doesn't matter. It's all you."

"And the thought of me is that painful?" She bit her lip.

"Excruciating."

"I had no idea."

He reached out and grabbed her hand. He didn't speak right away. Instead, he stroked her hand with his thumb and laced his fingers with hers. A small smile tugged at his lips.

"We don't have to do anything you don't want to do," he finally said. "We can go slow, or we don't have to do anything at all." The man had already waited six years. He was a paragon of patience.

"And if I said I didn't want to wait? If I didn't want to go slow?" She bit her lip. If he needed time, then she'd give him that, but she very much doubted that was the case, and she sure as Odin didn't want to wait a second longer.

Lincoln squeezed her hand at the same time he shut his eyes, like he couldn't believe she just said that.

"Is this the torment you mentioned?" she asked.

"I think you're trying to kill me."

Juni groaned and sat back in the couch. "I was trying to have sex with you. Fuck. I do suck at—"

Lincoln's mouth silenced hers. His lips and his tongue devoured her in the most glorious way, and she just hung on. Threading her fingers through his silky dark hair, she arched into his body. Her magic lashed out with anticipation, flooding the room and soaking into Lincoln's skin.

He shuddered and pulled back.

"Sorry. I can't seem to stop it when I'm with you," she said.

"Don't you dare stop." Gaze wild, he leaned in and

kissed her again, slowly, leisurely, moving away from her mouth to explore her face and neck. He grabbed the hem of her shirt and paused long enough to pull the clothing from her body.

With his mouth back on her skin, she ran her hands all over him. Anything she could reach, she touched. The taut back muscles, the flexed forearms that prevented him from crushing her with his weight. His butt. His gloriously rock-hard ass.

Everything she could get her greedy hands on, she groped. She'd wanted to touch him for years.

Lincoln's betrayal when they were teenagers had broken something inside her. She'd tried to see things from his point of view. He'd been a kid, sure, but that didn't excuse how he'd thought selfishly of himself and his mother and how to make their lives better the quick and easy way instead of getting a job and working hard. He didn't think about what would happen to her once he arranged for the hyenas to abduct her.

He hadn't thought about how it would break her heart to find out he'd only asked her out to set her up.

Those things alone were enough to turn Lincoln into her mortal enemy.

Yet, he wasn't.

He'd confessed how the part he played in her abduction was his greatest shame. He'd spent time in her sister's dungeon, then as her punching bag during training sessions with Rourke. He became her protector and spent years in the shadows atoning for the mistake he made when he was fifteen.

Juni had forgiven him a long time ago, though she'd only realized the truth more recently.

But Lincoln's actions made it clear he hadn't fully forgiven himself.

And right now, he atoned by making her body sing.

He removed her clothes slowly, leisurely, as if unwrapping a present and trying to savour each moment.

She pushed him back before he got to her underwear. "Why aren't you naked?"

Without a word, he stood up and tore his clothes from his body, flinging them over his shoulder before climbing back on the couch to lay beside her in his boxers. He kissed her again, and again and again until her head swam, and her body ached with need.

He wrapped her legs around his waist and sat up, bringing her with him. His erection pressed into her core and stirred an ache deep within her. Her heart pounded. Her breathing became shallow and rushed.

He stood, carrying her weight while tracing her jawline with his mouth,

"What are you doing?" she managed to ask, finding it hard to breathe.

"Finding a bed. I don't want our first time to be on Bane's couch. He could come back at any time." He pursed his lips. "I'd rather wait to get flower petals and champagne or whatever else you'd want to make it special."

"He said not to wait up. I doubt he'll return before morning." She snorted and grabbed his face with both hands so he couldn't look away. "And I just want you."

His expression softened.

"You make it special." She leaned in and kissed him. "And you're not taking me to my room here. There's a creepy fake fish hanging on the wall that sings and looks at you. Bane has it spelled for motion to trigger it."

Lincoln's face screwed up almost comically. "He really is evil."

He set her back on the couch and looked down at her. When he didn't do anything, she reached behind her back and popped the clasp to her bra.

His eyes widened.

She slipped out of the straps and tossed the bra to the floor. "You looked like you needed some encouragement."

His gaze flashed, reflecting the flames from the fireplace and his own mischief. "Is that so?"

"Mmhmm." She leaned forward and pressed her lips to his.

He groaned, quickly taking control of the kiss to the point of leaving her breathless. He kissed his way down her body, sliding off her underwear as he went. He looked at her as if she were the most beautiful person in the world, as if he couldn't quite believe he was there, between her legs with her naked in front of him.

She couldn't quite believe it either.

Completely naked and exposed, she'd expected to feel more vulnerable and shy, but that wasn't the case at all. She felt safe and secure with Lincoln. And right now, she was also very much in need of his body on hers. She reached up and pulled him down. He groaned but instead of stealing her mind away with his dizzying kisses, he pulled back enough so he could look at her while he shucked off his boxers and dug out a condom from his pants' pocket. Slowly, still studying her face with ferocious need, he unwrapped the condom and rolled it on. His muscles tensed and contracted, he moved with that familiar efficiency from hours of training.

She held her breath the entire time.

Lincoln's gaze spoke of want and need, but also something else, something deeper and a million times more powerful. She reached up and caressed his face.

"You're sure?" he asked, his voice raspy.

She nodded.

He pushed into her, his eyes widening.

Not taking his gaze away for a second, he worked his way in. It hurt, and then...it didn't. He paused, hovering above her, with his entire length inside her, filling her in a way she never thought possible.

"I want to hear it," he said.

"Hear what?"

"That you're mine."

"Lincoln..."

"You're mine." His gaze flashed.

"What about you?"

"I've been yours for years, Juni. I'll always be yours." He thrust, and the pleasure of the movement pulsed through her body. "I've been waiting for you to realize that."

More warmth spread through her body.

"You're mine. Say it." He thrust again. "Not Bane's. Not Rourke's. Mine."

She cupped the side of his face with her hand again. "I'm yours."

He dropped his head into her neck, holding her tightly as a shudder ran through his body, as if her words somehow broke a spell over his body. He kissed her face and her neck and then he began to move. "You won't regret it."

He'd never betray her again.

She already knew that, but his words sent warmth flooding her chest. He pumped into her, each thrust stoking an out-of-control wildfire. Fun? This wasn't fun. This was exquisite torture, and a pleasure she never knew existed. Lincoln continued to torment her body while he also proved without words that she was everything to him.

"Mine." She gripped his hair and lost herself in the waves of pleasure.

# CHAPTER 19

"Why do sloths never kiss on the first date?"
(Dramatic pause)
"They like to take it slow."

— JUNI'S DAD

J uni woke up with her face stuck to Lincoln's
bare chest and a crick in her neck. At some
point in the night, Lincoln had grabbed the
sheets from the fish room to cover them. She
peeled her cheek from his skin and rolled onto her
back, stretching her neck side to side and wincing.

Lincoln rolled onto his side, his thigh slipping over
her leg. He brushed some of her curls from her face.
Her hair probably looked like a bird's nest.

"You're beautiful in the morning," he said, his voice

low and more growly than normal. His hair had that tussled beach look, and his expression lacked his usual guarded expression. Dark circles lined the underside of his eyes.

She reached up and splayed her hand to cup his cheek. "You look exhausted."

He flashed her a wide smile. "I slept better last night than I have in years."

"So I don't always torment you?"

"Oh no. That's a constant struggle."

She snorted because she was classy like that.

Lincoln's expression softened. "How are you feeling?"

"Amazing," she said, and she meant it. Her body still tingled with the echoes of pleasure. Minus the stiff neck, she felt rested and relaxed.

Lincoln hesitated, a little pink tinging his cheeks. "Are you...sore?"

A little, but she wasn't telling him that. He might try to coddle her or withhold more sex. She had plans for him. "Nope."

He leaned in and whispered. "Liar."

"Okay. I'm a little sore."

He moved his hand to run his fingertips along her hip and thigh. "I'll kiss it better later."

Heat spread through her body. She'd like that a lot.

Tingling in the air interrupted whatever Lincoln planned to say next. He stiffened before quickly withdrawing his hand to pull the sheet up above her chest.

"What the fuck is going on?" Bane stepped out of the portal, letting it close behind him.

His gaze scanned the room, snagging on Juni and widening. His nostrils flared, and his eyes bled out to all black. He pinched the bridge of his nose and spun around to give them his back. "You have a fucking room."

"With a creepy fish."

Bane's shoulders tensed. "Get showered and dressed."

"Why?" She liked Lincoln's plan a lot better.

"We're off to see your sister."

Guess whatever Bane wanted to speed up had worked.

Juni exchanged a look with Lincoln. Maybe this meeting would be a good thing. Maybe it would be bad. But nothing could take last night away from either of them.

# CHAPTER 20

"I don't trust stairs."
(Dramatic pause)
"They're always up to something."

— JUNI'S DAD

Juni stepped out of the red smoky portal after Bane with Lincoln following right behind her. He'd insisted on coming to the meeting as well. Bane hadn't put up much of an argument. Her plans to wear him down, one annoyance at a time, was working.

Juni chose to wear the fae armour Bane had set out for her while muttering something about representing his court.

She'd pulled on the metal armour, suspiciously

light with the lingering smell of magic. Raven was going to be so pissed. That woman always got envious of armour. Though Raven could wear whatever she wanted, wearing less for shifting into her conspiracy made more sense. Despite the revealing nature of her signature battle bra, Raven wore it for practical reasons.

Lincoln reached out and clasped Juni's hand. She'd never grow tired of this—his silent presence his unwavering support.

The ceiling to her sister's grand hall opened to the night sky and natural red moonlight shone down. The fortress was built with pillars and walls of black brick and flooring of midnight granite. Crows, ravens, magpies, and the occasional blue jay watched them with beady eyes from where they perched on the walls surrounding the open hall, but instead of creeping Juni out, their presence comforted her. Raven and her oldest brother, Bear, had a special connection with corvids. More birds present meant more strength, and if tonight's showing was any indication, Raven had amassed a lot of power.

Raven sat on her throne of metal feathers. She wore the battle bra and a deep scowl.

Cole and Rourke stood behind her. Cole wore his black matte fae armour whereas Rourke had opted for the supple leather armour favoured by assassins. Neither of them looked happy to see Bane, but that was hardly unexpected.

Nobody liked Bane.

The name Bane might mean "glorious defender" in some countries, but the noun referred to anything that caused harm, ruin, or death. Given his proclivity to incite violence, his mother aptly named him.

"I hope you haven't wasted my time summoning me here. There is only one offer I will accept," Bane said.

Raven paused long enough to make Juni nervous. Her older sister's ability to improvise and survive eclipsed her own, but Bane took manipulation to the next level.

"Are you sure about that?" Raven finally answered.

Juni knew that smirk. Along with Raven's tendency to get distracted by shiny things, her tell was the reason she always lost playing poker with the family. Raven had an ace up the sleeve and itched to use it.

"What if I have a better offer?" Raven asked.

"I'll humour you by listening." Bane rested his hand on the hilt of his sword.

Juni frowned. He wouldn't draw the weapon. At least she didn't think he would. Bane didn't make empty threats. Maybe he didn't do it on purpose. Or maybe he had a tell of his own.

Juni narrowed her eyes.

"Tell me about this deal and why I shouldn't try to kill you where you sit while I use your sister as a shield," Bane said.

Raven looked ready to tear off the Lord of War's head. She wouldn't of course because of Juni.

Hopefully, Raven saw through this act. Bane was intentionally trying to bait her.

Why?

What was he up to?

Standing around, uselessly, while she watched her sister potentially walk into a trap grated every single one of Juni's nerves.

"Well, out with it." Bane tapped his foot while Raven seethed.

"You will release Juni from her bond." Raven lifted her chin to compete her defiant look.

"This is getting tiresome. But I'll play. Why should I do that?"

A look of satisfaction zinged through their bond before Bane shut it down.

"You'll do that because it will be a fair exchange."

Bane frowned but the hand on his sword hilt relaxed. "For what?"

"You mean for whom."

Raven's words settled over the courtroom like a death knell.

Juni blanched at her sister. What in Odin's blue balls had her sister done?

"For your son," Raven said.

Juni straightened. Her sister was many things, but a child killer wasn't one of them. She'd never harm an innocent child. Never. Not even for Juni. Raven lacked that kind of ruthlessness.

Unless...

She glanced at Bane and caught the smug tug on his lips. Maybe this was what Bane meant about speeding things up and giving Raven motivation.

Bane wanted Raven to bring down the barrier controlling the movement between the realms, but her sister had already offered to give him what he wanted if he released Juni. He'd passed on that deal. He must be after something more.

But what?

Now that he'd successfully motivated Raven, what would he ask for?

Bane barked out a laugh. He had a nauseating big laugh. One that filled the room.

Now she was thoroughly confused. If he wanted to motivate Raven into threatening his child's life...

Wait a minute.

Bane's son?

Bane had a kid?

The last time she'd seen Raven, her older sister was closing the Kayden Smith case. How had Raven managed to sneak in finding an unknown mystery child between the Kayden case and troll visits?

Unless...unless they were somehow related.

Kayden's mom looked like the woman in Bane's framed picture. Did that mean...

Juni's brain scrambled to connect the dots.

Holy shit.

Kayden Smith was Bane's son?

The Lord of War finally stopped laughing. "Oh *Rayray*. You continue to find ways to surprise me."

Yet...yet Bane wasn't surprised at all.

"You know what I like about ravens?" Bane asked.

"No, but I'm guessing you're going to tell me."

"They're resourceful," Bane answered without hesitation. "They're survivors."

Raven looked exhausted. Juni wanted to tell her to rest, to not stress out and to let Juni find her own way out of this mess. Raven shouldn't be doing all this work in her condition.

Juni glanced at Bane, wanting to smack the smug smile off his face. Did he know Raven was pregnant?

A heavy weight sunk in her stomach. Please, please don't let Bane find out.

"Will you agree to the deal or not?" Raven asked.

Juni held her breath.

"No."

"No?" Raven repeated.

"I said what I said," Bane replied.

Juni let out an exasperated breath. She'd known better than to hope...yet she had.

"I have your son and your lover held captive. I could return your son to Christian Smith and let him use your son's life and the dark fae magic running through his veins to puncture a hole through the barrier and establish a path to the Realm of Light. A path you will not have access to. A path that will undermine whatever twisted plans you have for the Mortal Realm."

Okay, then. Clearly, Juni had missed a lot while she and Lincoln lost their V cards on Bane's couch.

Kayden most definitely had to be Bane's son, and Christian Smith, the man who everyone thought was Kayden's biological father, intended to use Kayden for a connection between the Realm of Light and the Mortal Realm.

Juni stilled.

That sounded very similar to what a bunch of roller groups she'd run across in a previous investigation were trying to do.

Coincidence?

Maybe.

But coincidences rarely occurred in her line of work.

"You won't do that," Bane said to Raven, interrupting Juni's thought.

"Why not?" Raven asked.

"You're too soft to sacrifice an innocent boy. You won't give him to that sorry excuse of a human, and you certainly won't hurt or harm him yourself."

The pieces clicked together. Bane didn't mean or intend to motivate Raven to actually kill the child. He knew she'd never do it. He just needed to provide her with enough incentive to actually threaten the child.

Everything led up to this moment, but Juni still had so many questions.

"For these sorts of deals to work," Bane continued. "I have to believe you'll actually go through with your threats."

"You seem confident I won't stoop that low to protect my sister. Who's also innocent, by the way."

Lincoln froze beside her and clutched her hand.

"Not the way these two have been at it, she's not." Bane smirked.

Heat infused her face. He did not just say that. Please tell her, he didn't just say that.

The red tint to Lincoln's cheeks told her she hadn't imagined anything. The Lord of War had outed her sex life to her sister's entire court.

Juni bit back a hysterical laugh.

Raven looked ready to murder Bane on her behalf.

"You won't do it," Bane said again, circling back to Raven's morals as if he hadn't just humiliated Juni. "Even if you tried, your entire family would stop you. Morals can be so pesky like that."

He wasn't wrong.

"Free my sister and I'll free your son," Raven said.

"Saying it in a slightly different way won't change the results," Bane said.

Juni held back a deep sigh. Getting out of this bond today had been a nice, tempting thought.

"I might not have it in me to kill your son," Raven admitted. "But I'm not above keeping him from you."

Yes! Juni bit back the fist pump and tried to keep her face neutral.

Bane stiffened where he stood beside her, and his hand curled into a fist.

But...

But he had to have seen this coming.

"It's a fair deal," Raven said.

"I'm giving up my caomhnóir who's your sister. You're only giving up my son. He has no special value to you nor a special place in your life."

Juni snorted. His words implied she had a *special place* in his life and was, therefore, more of a sacrifice to give up. What a load of crap.

Raven waited, and Juni held her breath, Bane had come to barter, and that statement let him move the conversation in his desired destination—where he asked for what he really wanted.

Maybe.

Bane was cagey as fuck so this might all be another simple step in his master plan instead of his end game.

"I will release your sister from the caomhnóir bond and return her to you, alive and unharmed. In exchange, you will return my son to me, alive and unharmed and assist me in destroying the Lighters."

Hope zinged across Juni's skin. Bane had finally offered a deal to release her, but his wording rang little warning bells in her head.

"It's a good deal, Raven," Bane said. "Agree to it."

"I will," Raven said. "But...why?"

There it was. The reason Bane's words bothered her. Why would the Lord of War require her sister's assistance to take down some extremist group made up of regs?

"I need your help," Bane said.

Juni nearly fell over.

"Can you repeat that?" Raven asked.

And thank Odin's left nut Raven asked because Juni had begun to worry she'd lost her mind.

Bane snarled in response but didn't elaborate.

Juni's mind reeled while Bane and Raven worked out the specific wording of the agreement and swore a fae oath. She kept going over their words. What was she missing? Should she stop this? Bane had used her as a pawn in his game. He'd used her, and she couldn't figure out exactly why or how. Did this all lead to the Lighters? And if so, she had a lot more questions. Why would the Lord of War need Raven to launch an attack? Why Raven, specifically? It didn't fit a revenge plot.

The entire time Bane spoke his binding oath to Raven, a small smile tugged at his lips.

He'd achieved his goal, and he'd used her and his own son to achieve it.

After the oath pulled the fae knot tight, Bane turned to her. Raven had negotiated for the bond to be dissolved first.

Juni licked her lips.

Finally, she'd be free. She'd expected it to take years.

If only she could figure out the true cost.

Bane reached out and held her face in both his hands. Instead of feeling cold like how she'd imagined, his warm skin pressed against her cheeks, the hard callouses from sword handling scratched a little.

Rough hands.

A fighter's hands.

Yet he was surprisingly gentle and that bothered her more somehow. In fact, he hadn't mistreated her at all. She'd bonded her life to this dark fae lord, and she didn't really know or understand him.

"Oh, Juni," he crooned. "Our time was short and sweet."

And it hadn't stopped him from getting what he wanted.

"When your lover has lived his measly reg life and his body is a dried husk, come find me. We could have some fun, you and I."

Juni's stomach sunk. Her heart convulsed. His words played in her head over and over again.

Lincoln's reg life...because humans and shifters had shorter lifespans than the fae.

And she was no longer just a shifter. She'd embraced her light fae heritage, which meant...

Before she could crumple to the floor, Bane reached into her soul with his corrosive dark fae power.

*You will always be mine,* his voice whispered in her head.

Without waiting for a response, he severed the bond between them.

Pain shot from her chest.

Bane's essence withdrew, and her body ached from the loss. Her only power flared up as if to chase down Bane's. When it finally returned to her core without the company of Bane's bond, she felt empty and a little less whole.

But also free.

She was free now.

# EPILOGUE

"Do you know what they say about finding love on the
internet?"
(Dramatic pause)
"It's virtually impossible."

— JUNI'S DAD

J uni didn't remember much after Bane tore his
bond from her soul. She vaguely recalled the
hiss of pain, Lincoln's arms wrapping around
her and the press of a portal's magic on her
skin.

Her eyes fluttered open to find Lincoln's face about
a foot away from hers, his gaze searching, his brows
pinched.

They lay on their sides facing each other in her bed. The familiar scents wrapped around her. She was home. Safe.

"Did you know?" she asked.

Lincoln reached out and lifted a lock of curly hair from her face, tucking the mass behind her ear.

"I don't care." His voice was deep and growly.

"You're going to grow old...and I'm not." Another pain stabbed at her chest.

Lincoln somehow managed a half shrug from his position. "I'm a reg, Juni. I was always going to grow old."

"But I'm not. Not anymore, anyway."

"Juni..." He caressed her face with his fingertips, following her brow line, nose, cheekbones and finally her lips. "I love you."

She sucked in a breath.

"And yes, I will only have one lifetime to love you, but I was only ever going to have one lifetime. So for me, not much has changed. I wish we could grow old together, but instead, the woman I love will carry me through time with her thoughts and memories and hopefully, in her heart long after I'm gone. That's immortality in a way."

"But—"

He leaned in and silenced her with a kiss. He took her breath away and a little of her heart, too. Okay, a lot of her heart. He made her body sing, and the weird emptiness in her soul from the loss of Bane's bond didn't feel so empty any more.

"All this means is we have time," Lincoln said. "Lots of time."

She shoved his chest. "That's not funny."

"It's kind of funny." Lincoln winked. "Your near immortality doesn't bother me. Does being with a lowly reg bother you? You're the one who will have to say goodbye. I think that will be harder in a lot of ways."

"I don't give a shit if you're a reg as long as you're mine..." She kissed him back. "I love you, too."

He smiled, pressing his lips to hers again while pulling her closer. His familiar scent wound around her. Familiar and welcome. He smelled like iron and leather.

He smelled like home.

Light fae magic spread from her body and covered them like a blanket. An ancient fae song slipped from her mouth.

"Let me love you, Juni," he whispered against her lips. "Let me spend my short life loving you."

Her heart and head still hurt from the pain of their unknown future, a pain she could only imagine at the moment, a pain that threatened to break her into pieces. That was what losing Lincoln would cost. That would be the price of loving Lincoln.

And he was worth it.

He was worth everything.

\* \* \* \* \*

Thank you for reading

If you haven't read the Raven Crawford books yet
and want to know more of the story,
start with *Conspiracy of Ravens,*
a full length novel by J. C. Mckenzie

Recommended Reading order:

*Conspiracy of Ravens*
(Raven #1, Crawford Investigations #1)

*Nevermore*
(Raven #2, Crawford Investigations #2)

*Queen of Corvids*
(Raven #3, Crawford Investigations #3)

*From the Shadows*
(Juni #1, Crawford Investigations #5)

*Into the Fire*
(Juni #2, Crawford Investigations #6)

*Dark Legacy*
(Raven #4, Crawford Investigations #7)

Companion Stories:

*The Call of Corvids*
(Bear #1, Crawford Investigations #4)

*Embrace the Flame*
(Juni #3, Crawford Investigations #8)

# GLOSSARY OF TERMS

**Bear Crawford:** Juni's half-brother. Caller of Corvids. Raven's twin.

**Caomhnóir:** Pronounced "keevenoyr." A guardian blood sworn to protect fae nobility.

**Cole Camhanaich:** Full fae name is Beul na h-Oidhche gu Camhanaich (pronounced: Bee-al nuh huhee-khye guh Ca-van-eekh). Raven Crawford's husband and anam cara. Patron Fae of Assassins and Lord of Shadows, Son of Erebus born of Chaos.

**Dark fae:** Any fae from any of the realms within the Underworld.

**Hikaru:** Kitsune.

**Hōju:** A golden orb said to grant wishes in a time of need.

**Inari:** Japanese kami of grains, harvest, and agriculture. Juni's maternal great-grandmother.

**Lighters:** An organization comprised of roller groupies who are obsessed with the Realm of Light.

**Lincoln:** reg. Former classmate of Juni's and former prisoner in Raven's dungeons. Imprisoned for his part in Juni's abduction by a hyena shifter gang. Currently, Juni's sparring partner.

**Mike Crawford:** Juni's brother. Hacker, programmer, technology extraordinaire.

**Mortal:** Any inhabitant of the Mortal Realm. Note: All entities of all the realms can be killed, but this term is reserved for anyone who is not an Other. Used as a derogatory slur by Others.

**Other:** Any inhabitant NOT from the Mortal Realm. Any inhabitant from the Realm of Light, the Underworld or the Shadow Realm. Mortal, but not a mortal.

**Raven Crawford:** Juni's half-sister and Queen of Corvids. Bear's twin.

**Reg:** A "regular" human being from the Mortal Realm without any supernatural powers or skills.

**Regulators:** An organized group of regs who despise Others and hold meetings to bitch about the unfairness of life.

**ROL:** Realm of Light. An Other realm full of Rollers who look down on everyone else.

**Rollers:** Supernatural beings from the Realm of Light.

**Rourke:** Dark fae weapon-warper. Former member of Assassin's guild. Currently, Raven's life-bound guardian.

**Underworld:** An Other realm, often in direct conflict with the Realm of Light. Contains multiple, smaller realms, such as the realms of War and Lust.

# ACKNOWLEDGMENTS

I'd like to thank Patricia D. Eddy, J. E. Taylor, Wendy Passalent, Karilyn Bentley, and Nicole Flockton for beta reading, Anna L. Spies from Antra Luna Cover Designs (formerly Eerilyfair Designs) for the beautiful cover, Book Nook Nuts for the proofreading and Lara Parker for the editing.

I'd also like to thank my family, friends and readers for their support.

It may take a village to raise a child, but it takes a team of very patient, understanding individuals to support an author.

Thank you.

# ABOUT THE AUTHOR

J. C. McKenzie is a book loving, gumboot-wearing, unapologetic science geek. She predominantly writes urban fantasy and post-apocalyptic dystopian fantasy with strong romantic elements. When she's not spinning tales, she's in the classroom sharing her passion for science and mathematics while secretly warping the young, impressionable minds of our future to carry out her evil plans for world domination. She lives in the Pacific Northwest with her family.

## Visit her at jcmckenzie.ca

facebook.com/j.c.mckenzie.author

twitter.com/JC_McKenzie

instagram.com/j.c.mckenzie

tiktok.com/@jcmckenzieo

bookbub.com/authors/j-c-mckenzie